Crazy For You

Claire Applewhite

L & L Dreamspell
Spring, Texas

Cover and Interior Design by L & L Dreamspell

This is a work of fiction, and is produced from the author's imagination. People, places and things mentioned in this novel are used in a fictional manner.

ISBN: 978-1-60318-274-4

Library of Congress Control Number: 2010924125

Visit us on the web at www.lldreamspell.com

Published by L & L Dreamspell
Printed in the United States of America

ACKNOWLEDGEMENTS

A cruel tyrant or an elusive butterfly, love can be poison or candy. Consider "love at first sight." Phenomena or rubbish? What price is too high for the love of a lifetime? The popularity of internet dating sites suggests that people will pay—and pay—for a stab at such a love. Yet, plans and computers cannot predict or create chemistry. After all, people are not machines. Could it be that the love of a lifetime is disguised in a facade that does not match a "profile?" In the end, the heart knows what the mind does not.

The late mystery writer Ed McBain once reflected that, in his opinion, love or money were the only two motives for murder. In the story you are about to read, there is an overabundance of love and money—in all the wrong places.

I would like to thank those in my life who taught me what I know about love. My deepest gratitude to my dear family, my friends who contribute their time and resources to local charities, Dale McAdams and Terry Schumaier, my Airedales, Jack and Lola, and finally, my husband, Thomas Applewhite, M.D., my own "love at first sight."

Thank you to the faculty at Washington University, the L&L Dreamspell team, Linda Houle and Lisa Smith, my editor, Cindy Davis, and my multi-talented assistant, Lois Mans, for expertise, patience and confidence in my work. Their invaluable knowledge continues to guide me.

Now, on with the show!

Claire Applewhite
March, 2010

DEDICATION

For Tom

A ticking clock, the setting sun,
Once I walked alone.
Years ago and yesterday,
I took you for my own.

Winter, spring, summer, fall,
Our world goes 'round the sun.
Change, grow, harvest, plant,
You'll always be the One.

To our tomorrows,
Claire

One

Dan wouldn't have been sitting at the Cinnabar Club without Bunny Dingwerth. He sipped the fine wine and admired a gleaming chandelier. He was a smart enough guy. On a good day, a hard-worker, and on a better one, better looking than most. Still, he knew what thousands of smart, hard-working, good-looking guys didn't have.

"Danny?" Bunny giggled, and twined her hair through her slender fingers. Her straight, white teeth glistened in the glow of soft candlelight. "I'll be right back, Danny. I need to go to the little girls' room." She snatched her cute pink clutch purse, and pranced among the tables.

In that rare moment, Bunny piqued Dan's curiosity. Puzzled, he sat motionless while Bunny floated among the tables, first to one friend, and then another, to chat, chat, chat. For twenty minutes or so, she'd posed by his side in stony silence—punctuated by peals of silly giggles—and now, it was chat, chat, chat.

Time for another glass of wine. He inspected the rolls in the breadbasket and chose a brown one with sesame seeds. He didn't like rolls, especially ones with seeds. He wasn't hungry. Yet, he nibbled, chewed, swallowed, his eyes glazed with regret. What bothered him so much?

He sliced a corner from a pat of butter and smeared it on a tattered piece of bread. After all, things were going well, weren't they? He was Vice-President in charge of something—

well nothing really—at his father-in-law's printing company. They had a perfect little—well not so little, June Senior wouldn't allow *little*—so it was a perfect *larger* house nice and close to June Senior. Bunny had lots of time for tennis at the Cinnabar Tennis Club, and now, he had lots of new Bunny friends. Why then, did he feel so confused?

Poverty and shame haunted Dan's youth. Now, his wealth exceeded any and all expectations. A football scholarship and marriage to a future heiress won him the future of his Plan. All he needed to do was savor it, and smile The Smile. How Bunny loved that smile—the one she said made him look like Tom Cruise. He took another sip of wine, and another, followed by yet another one. He floated, high above the chaos. Maybe he could fly…

"Ready to order yet, Mr. Hunter?"

Dan glanced up to see Rocco, his favorite waiter. *What a relief!* "You know how it is, Rocco. Waiting for the new wife." Rocco winked.

"How long you been married now, Mr. Hunter?"

Dan smiled The Smile. "Almost a year now."

"Ah, newlyweds." Rocco nodded. "I'll be back in a few minutes. Anything else I can get for you sir?"

"No, nothing. I'll just…wait…right—"

"Sir?" The clinking glasses, the scraping silverware, the buzzing conversation—all noise had been drenched by the sight of *her*—the lady in the open doorway luminous in the beams of a full August moon.

"Mr. Hunter," Rocco said. "Are you not feeling well?"

Dan had never seen a woman so exquisite, not in all his thirty years. Quite simply, she was everything Bunny was not. With her dark hair, dark, almond-shaped eyes, and sensuous mouth, she might have been Ava Gardner, his favorite movie star from the Forties.

Rocco leaned closer to him and whispered. "You know her, sir?"

Dan shook his head. He struggled to smile at the exotic stranger. He couldn't.

"She is very beautiful, eh?" Rocco said. "But, a little too late for you—eh, my friend?"

Rocco chuckled, and nudged Dan in the ribs. "And look! The Mrs. She is right on time." Entranced, Dan turned to see Bunny, prancing across the dining room toward him. Her slick lip-gloss shined like new patent leather.

"Hi Danny!" Bunny giggled, and her button-like nose scrunched. She pressed her cheek against his, and nuzzled his lips. "I'll bet you were wondering where I was." A cold stare glowed from her eyes. "Or, were you?"

"What? What did you say, Bunny?" Dan's desperate gaze scanned the room for That Woman.

"Wondering about *me*, Danny. Don't you know what I mean?"

"Sure. Sure, I do."

Dan knew one thing. This heady rush of magic felt new and intoxicating—and dangerous. He liked it and he craved it. But, he needed much more.

Later, in their darkened bedroom, Dan's feelings obsessed him. He studied the dancing shadows on the wall, bathed in the moonlight. Unaware, Bunny slumbered beside him. This was crazy. That Woman didn't fit his Plan, if indeed it still existed. Until today, he thought he knew Daniel Hunter, where he was headed, and how he would arrive. He'd pulled it off too. Then, beneath the light of a full moon, "she" walked into the Cinnabar Club and changed everything.

Be rational, Dan, it's just a woman. Lust had overcome him, that's all. He had to forget this madness. He tossed against the sheets to face the windows. The white moonlight startled him. He had never seen a moon so full and luminous.

He lay on his back now, staring at the ceiling fan. This craziness wouldn't end, he decided, until one thing happened. He must find that Woman. She'd come to the Cinnabar Club to meet someone. Who was that person? Rocco might know. If he didn't, he could find out.

Finally, Dan Hunter had a Plan. He slept, wrapped in a white, bright blanket of light.

Two

The Dingwerth Mansion
Friday Evening, around six o'clock

"Please pass the mashed potatoes, Dan." June smiled now, her little yellow teeth outlined by a thin, red mouth. "I just love mashed potatoes, don't you? But, not with too much salt, not too much butter, not too much milk, and heaven help us, not too much pepper. I mean, you can just have too much of anything, don't you think so, Dan?"

Dan flashed The Smile. He knew his perfect white teeth, devilish green eyes, and impish grin could charm a cobra—Tom Cruise at his finest. Once again, like so many times before this one, he charmed June Senior. Perfect. He passed the mashed potatoes, enrobed by a massive bone china thing that he couldn't wait to unload. It, like anything and everything Dingwerth, was just "too much."

Only two years ago, Dan couldn't have pictured life with the Dingwerths. He'd done very well, he told himself. Just look at the two of them, he and Bunny. Her real name was June after her mother, but everyone called her Bunny, go figure. A new job, a new home, and a new boss, with a most eligible, well-connected, young—did he mention rich?—daughter. Well yes, Bunny was rich, very. But he hadn't allowed himself to be bought, absolutely not. He felt The Stare. What did June Senior want that she didn't already have?

"So Dan," she said, just before she gulped a ball of mashed potatoes that traveled the length of her crepe-draped neck, "when are you and Bunny going to give me a grandchild? I can't wait until I'm a Granny, or maybe Grams, or should I say Gramma? Well, it's important, you know, because I'll be seeing little June or Giles everyday, won't I, and..."

Once again, Dan smiled. "Actually, Bunny and I have been talking, and well, I thought she would have mentioned it...Bunny, did you tell June about the sportscaster job offer I received last month? You know, the one we were thinking about taking? Bunny? Remember Amarillo?"

"Nooo..." Bunny whispered and turned her face to one side, away from her mother's view. "Danny, really. Not now. Mommy isn't up to it."

"Young Daniel," said Giles, "what's all this? Why would we or anyone else be interested in a sportscaster named—what was it, Daniel-Armadillo, you say? My God." Giles gulped brandy from a goblet and shook his narrow, balding head. "Can't imagine it. Well Daniel, go on then, go on."

June's mouth quivered and gaped. The fine creases caked her mouth with scarlet lip-stickies. She simply stared at the mashed potatoes and gulped.

Bunny's lip-gloss glistened like new aluminum foil. "Daddy, Danny is talking about a job, silly. He'd be a sportscaster in Amarillo. It's really a step up for him."

"But Bunnykins, Amarillo is in Texas. That's really quite a commute for young Daniel. But, if he thinks he can do it, why, well...I can't imagine...whatever... Giles gazed onto the expansive lawn that ended at the massive iron gates, the ones embellished with the massive golden D. "Texas is quite the drive."

"So that's where Amarillo is," Bunny said. "Well, Danny likes his car, don't you Danny? And he really loves to drive it."

June Senior stared at Daniel with the gaze of an executioner. Dan sipped some iced tea and braced himself for the brewing soliloquy, the one that would swirl like a Texas tornado. He knew he shouldn't have taken the seat beside June Senior. Why had he done just that? Because the Junebug told him to do it, that's why. Now, he would pay for his compliance. He reached across the table and patted his wife's hand, the one that sported the diamond that June Senior had selected, the one Mr. Dingwerth had financed, and smiled The Smile.

Giles swirled the last of the brandy in his snifter. He seemed deep in thought. Finally, he shattered the tense silence with a voice that boomed from the head of the table. "I'm quite sure young Daniel here," he said, with a cold-eyed glimpse in Dan's direction, "did not intend disrespect toward my wife and Bunny's mother. Did you, Daniel?"

Dan felt like a caged animal. He couldn't even smile The Smile. "Excuse me," he said. "I'm going to step out for a moment to get a little air." Maybe a whole lot of it, he thought. Maybe a whole country full of it.

A muffled chorus of whispers resounded; Dan heard them and he didn't care. He shuffled from the dining room. His face felt scalded. The old place felt like a maze. He stumbled down a long corridor now, terrazzo floor beneath his shaky feet, the plaster walls covered in family portraits featuring God Knows Who. A draft brushed his cheek, and the air felt cool against his flushed skin. He gripped a suspicious doorknob on the right, and discovered a broom closet. *Nope, keep walking.*

A light beamed under a heavy wooden door farther down, on the left side of the hall. Could it be? Suddenly, the door cracked. A small, stooped woman appeared in the dim doorway, dressed in a faded black dress. A frayed white apron covered the dress, stiff with starch. "Help you, sir?" she said in a meek, yet suspicious tone.

Dan almost burst into laughter. *Help me? Help me? No one can help me.* "Just looking for the bathroom," he said.

Somehow, this diminutive woman had succeeded in making him feel like a fool. For this, he could have remained seated beside June Senior. This woman half-frowned at him, staring while she spoke. "You shouldn't be in this part of the house, didn't you know? The bathroom is in the other wing, by the patio. Come, I'll show you."

Dan followed the small woman's short, clipped steps down the cavernous hallway. Her stooped back and furrowed face belied the flight of her feet. At the end of the corridor, she turned and gestured toward an open doorway. "A bathroom?"

Dan nodded. "Thanks, um... Excuse me, what is your name?"

The woman bowed her head. "Felicity, Sir."

"Felicity. I'll remember that. By the way, my name is Dan. Dan Hunter."

Felicity's expression changed, ever so subtly. A knowing look came over her, one he didn't understand, nor could he explain her reply.

"I know who you are," she said.

The Hunter Bedroom—Later That Evening

Dan lay on his back, staring at the ceiling fan, wondering how he could endure decades of Sunday dinners with June Senior— June Senior and her mashed potatoes. Would he become Giles Dingwerth? His gut wrenched. NO. No, he would not. God! He just had to find that ravishing woman.

Well, Rocco might know where to find her. If he didn't, Rocco could figure it out. She'd come to the Cinnabar to meet someone. If only he knew that much, it might calm his jangled nerves. For a little extra *dinero*, Rocco could work a little bit harder. Now, Dan felt relieved, and yet, oddly agitated. At least now though, he had a Plan. Almost immediately, he felt much better.

He tossed against the sheets, first facing the windows, then, Bunny's side of the bed. For the first time Dan stared at the bleached, golden hair streaming down her back and wondered about her nickname. On one of their first dates, she told him she had been named after her mother, June Senior. So, why did everyone call her Bunny? He wondered if Bunny knew. June Senior knew, but after today, she probably wouldn't tell him, at

least for awhile. Well, it didn't matter. It just didn't matter.
He rolled over and fell into a deep sleep.

The Following Morning—The Hunter Kitchen

"Danny," Bunny said, "do you remember the first time we met?"

She lounged at the breakfast table, wrapped in a light pink chenille robe, her golden hair gathered in a loose ponytail at the back of her head. Plush white bunny slippers adorned her pink, pedicured feet. Her cereal bowl brimmed with Lucky Charms cereal, and she poked at the marshmallow moons and hearts with her spoon, frowning at—what? What had captured her attention?

Dan couldn't possibly fathom what went through that fluffy mind sometimes, and this was one of those moments. He sipped at the steaming coffee in his bone china cup. Okay, he would at least try to humor her, but his mind, he had to admit, was elsewhere. "Sure I do. How could I ever forget it?"

Bunny scrunched her nose and scooped a heaping spoonful of Lucky Charms into her perfect pink mouth. "I wondered." Dan took another cautious sip and stared at her. *Bunny wondered?*

"To this day, Bunny, it remains the most embarrassing day of my life. You know that. Do you think I liked starting the first day of my college career with my screwed up football scholarship they said they didn't give me, and twenty dollars to my name? And then, to have the guy at the registration table say he would cancel my registration unless I could get it all straightened out, or better yet, why don't I just write him a big fat check, right there in front of everyone, including you. I'm not sure why or how you ever wanted to have anything to do with someone like me after that. Actually, now that I think about it, 'how we met' isn't one of my happiest memories of all time, especially of us."

Now, Bunny giggled. A line of milk dribbled from the corner of her mouth. Dan glared at her. Because…well, because it almost seemed like Bunny had deliberately set out to wound him, but…but, that was absurd. Bunny wasn't clever enough to hurt him. He wiped his mouth with his napkin and rose to face another day with Giles Dingwerth. His empty briefcase rested beside his white enameled chair. Now, he bent to grab it, and as he stood up, he glimpsed the smirk on Bunny's face. If he didn't know better, he'd think she had mocked him. But, he decided, no. That couldn't be possible.

"Something wrong, Danny?" she said. The grandfather clock in the foyer chimed eight times.

"No," he said. "I mean, why were you wondering if I remember how we met? Why would it matter now?"

With a sly gleam in her eyes, Bunny crossed her long, tanned legs. The robe slipped apart, exposing a length of firm thigh. She flipped her top foot, and the beady bunny eyes on the slippers bounced. "Rocco called last night. He said he had the information you wanted. And I said, Rocco…from the Club, Rocco? And he said, yes, Mrs. Hunter. But you know Danny, I didn't like the way I kept feeling he wanted to hang up on me."

"Bunny, did Rocco call the house?" Dan's anger surged.

"No, he called your cell. You were in the bathroom, and it kept ringing right there on the nightstand, so I answered it."

"You shouldn't have done that."

"Okay." Bunny uncrossed her legs and frowned. "Danny?"

His hand on the doorknob, Dan sighed. Almost made it—almost. "Yes, Bunny. What is it?"

"Who was that woman at the Club last night?"

Instantly, his morning coffee became heartburn. He wanted to say "what woman?" but to play dumb to Bunny's "smarts" was out of the question, at least in his mind; however confused it might be at the moment. No, he had a better idea. He would know her. He was a genius, that's what he was. "She was in my high school class. A long, long time ago. She looks exactly the same, though."

"Really? What's her name?" Now, Bunny studied the back of the cereal box. The connect-the-dots puzzle appeared to fascinate her. Dan snatched a ballpoint pen from the inside pocket of his suit coat. *Seized the moment!*

"Here," he said, offering the pen to his wife. "I think I know just what you want."

Without a glance, Bunny accepted the pen and began connecting the dots. "I want to know her name, Danny."

Think fast. He had it. "It's Ava. Ava Gardner. Ever heard of her?"

Bunny shook her ponytail. She continued to trace. "Nope."

"Didn't think so." Dan pecked her pink, fair-skinned cheek and turned to leave, taking a deep breath. "Enjoy your day, darling."

Finally, Dan was on his way, cruising on the highway towards Dingwerth Distinguished Designs, aka DDD.

"Never forget the three D's, Dan," Mr. Dingwerth had told him the night that he and Bunny announced their engagement. "That's my credo."

At the time, Dan thought that perhaps the three D's stood for something other than Dingwerth Distinguished Designs, a ruse for some clever "insider" knowledge; but, as "the talk" unfurled, he decided Giles Dingwerth was not a deep man.

"Think you can remember that?" he had said, puffing on a cigar, his bushy eyebrows fluttering above his wire rimmed glasses when he spoke. Dan replied that he could.

He angled his black Porsche into his reserved parking spot and yanked the key from ignition. For a moment, he sat, frozen in thought. He hadn't quite deciphered the world of Giles Dingwerth, or for that matter, his daughter. Most of the time, their respective transparence seemed too simple to be genuine. Still, there were those rare moments when clarity struck. Dan pondered his dilemma: were Mr. Dingwerth and his daughter simple fools blessed with dumb luck, or quiet opportunists searching for the occasional big score?

Dan had a plan for nearly everything. He admired men with deliberate thoughts, words and actions. The fateful night at the Cinnabar had been the only meaningful exception in his entire life.

And now, he would call Rocco.

Three

"Shhh," Giles said, easing his pale feet onto the floor. "I thought I heard someone at the door." A quizzical look crossed her exotic face—the face of a model, a movie star.

"But who? It's so early, is it not?"

"No, Leila, it's later than you think. We overslept." A hasty rustling of sheets sifted through the door. A thin line of sunlight streamed through a crack in the heavy drapes. She flipped on the bedside lamp.

"Oh no, Giles, it's eight thirty! I'll miss my nine o'clock photo shoot."

"No, you won't. I'll send the car around for you. Just give them a quick call if you're worried."

She was in the tiny bathroom now with the water running. The creaky toilet flushed. "When can I see you again?" he asked.

Swathed in a white bath towel, Leila posed barefoot in the doorway. Even without makeup, without the delicious scarlet gown and all the dazzling jewelry, still exquisite. She pulled on a pair of tight jeans and a simple black T-shirt. With her dark hair pulled back and tinted sunglasses shading her sultry brown eyes, this Ava Gardner was breathtaking.

One thing Giles Dingwerth *knew*. He couldn't live without her. Whatever exorbitant price it took to keep her in his life, he would pay it willingly, more if necessary. A sharp knock at the door shattered his reverie. Giles barely twisted the knob. Startled, he pressed his ear to the faint opening. "Yes?" he asked, his voice a hoarse whisper.

"The car," the maid, Felicity, said. "It is waiting, Mr. Dingwerth." Mr. Dingwerth wasn't listening. His arms held Leila's lush body close to his own. His lips tasted the magic of hers. Another insistent knock broke the spell.

"Mr. Dingwerth?"

"Tomorrow?" Giles' face flushed with fresh desire.

"I'll call you." Leila rushed for the beckoning mahogany door.

"I'll be waiting, darling." He watched her from the wide window that faced the expansive front lawn, the one that bordered the long, twisted drive that led to the gates emblazoned with the gargantuan golden D's. Yes, just as Felicity as promised, there was the black Mercedes, waiting to ferry Leila to her first modeling assignment of the day. He smiled and turned away, confident that she would arrive on time. After all, Rocco sat behind the wheel.

Rocco stared straight ahead, not daring to brave a backward glance. Yes, she was beautiful…ah, breathtaking was the word, but then, the whole world had noticed that, had they not? Take Mr. Hunter last night, for example. Rocco almost laughed out loud at the thought of him. Now, there was a man who really had lost his breath.

"Take a right up here, please," said the glamorous woman.

Rocco glanced in the rear view mirror. He wondered if she would mind a little salsa music, eh? He didn't get to find out. He silenced the shrill cell phone on the second ring. "Rocco speaking," he said, eyes fixed on the winding, narrow road.

"Rocco, it's me, Dan Hunter."

Rocco couldn't have explained why, but instinctively, his voice lowered, his manner became a tad more guarded, and suddenly, he was intensely aware of his passenger's presence. Had the car in front of him not suddenly stopped, he would have missed her destination.

"One minute, sir." He jerked the car beside the curb. He glanced back at the lovely lady. "So sorry about the stop, there."

Without a word, she grabbed her purse and flung the car door wide before swinging one long leg onto the sidewalk. Rocco turned around and sighed. Yes, she was mad. He would certainly hear about this from Mr. Dingwerth. He checked his watch—8:56 a.m. Well, he'd gotten her there on time. He would be sure to remember that part, just in case. "Mr. Hunter, are you still there, sir?"

"Yes, I'm here. Look Rocco, what's going on? Can you talk or not?"

"Yes, yes. Now I can, sir."

"You can cut the sir stuff, Rocco. I'm younger than you."

"Yes, sir."

"Did you get the information? You know, about last night?"

"Oh yes. I tried to call you, but the wife…"

"Yes, the wife told me all about your little chat. From now on, what we say stays between us. Right?"

A tense pause lapsed.

"Right?"

"What's happened, Mr. Hunter?"

"What do you think has happened, Rocco? I've met someone. Now, who is she?"

The spicy scent of her perfume still clung to the backseat of the car. Rocco simply did not know what he should say or do.

"Well, do you know her or not?"

"Oh, I know her alright. But, there is one thing you should know, I think."

"What's her name, Rocco? Just tell me her name, for starters anyway."

"Her name is Leila. Leila Bolivar. She is from Venezuela. Caracas, I think."

"How do you know this?"

"Uh-oh." Rocco chuckled. "My sources are not part of our deal, do you not remember that?"

"Okay, okay. Does she speak English?"

"Yes." Again, Rocco laughed. "Do I speak English? Yes. I also speak Spanish. And, so does she. But, there is the one other thing."

"I should say so. Our deal included her phone number, remember?"

"Yes, I remember. That, I know."

"Okay." Rocco heard Dan take a deep breath on the other end of the line. Finally, he spoke in a gruff, low growl. "Rocco, what the hell is the problem?"

"There is still the one thing about her you should know."

Dan chuckled. "Nothing you can say is going to keep me from calling her. Nothing. I mean, what is it? Is she married or something?" Rocco cleared his throat. He had been dreading this moment. Now, it had arrived.

"Yes, sir."

"Married?"

"Yes, she is."

"Are you sure?"

"Yes, Mr. Hunter. To a wealthy businessman from Venezuela. You should be very, very careful, is my best advice."

"Venezuela? Why is she here?"

"She is a model. And, you should know something else too." To Rocco, Dan sounded furious now, maybe with him, he couldn't say why. He had done his job, had he not?

"What else is there? Can't you say something cheerful for a change, something that might give me a good laugh? I'll tell you, I could really use a good laugh today. Tell me something funny."

Rocco took a deep breath. Funny, eh? Did he dare? "Leila Bolivar is married, like I told you, Mr. Hunter. But she is a very busy lady. She has time on her hands, or used to, until the Cinnabar."

"Look, what are you trying to tell me?"

"I am trying to say that she came to the club to meet a date, Mr. Hunter."

"Did she?"

"What?"

"Meet him?"

"It would seem so. She was with him this morning."

"Well, I don't care who he is. That doesn't matter. I want to meet her."

"But Mr. Hunter..."

"Don't try to talk me out of this, Rocco. You can't. My mind's already made up. And don't go judging me, either. A deal is a deal. Now, meet me at the club at noon today. I'll be hanging around the dining room somewhere, looking for you. You give me the phone number, and I'll give you the money, and you'll keep your mouth shut, like we agreed. Everybody's happy. You and me, we call it even." Rocco cleared his throat.

"Yes, Mr. Hunter."

Rocco clicked off and sat in the car for a moment, deep in thought. In his mind, nothing about this deal even approached "even."

"Mommy?" Bunny giggled into the phone. "I'm off to the club to play some tennis. What? Well, it's Monday. Penny and Candy should be there, don't you remember? I could ask them. Who? Oh. Danny's fine. Well, I think so. He always looks that way, Mommy. He's fine, really." A few kisses into the phone and "bye."

Bunny headed for the shower. She didn't understand why June Senior worried so much about Danny's feelings. Danny didn't worry that much about June's, at least in Bunny's opinion. Besides, what more could Danny want, now that he had Bunny's money—oops!—she *meant* her perfect life, to share with her and of course, her wonderful Mommy.

She yanked the pink elastic band from her ponytail and hopped into the steamy shower. That's what she talked to Danny about this morning—because in her opinion, that's what she had to do every now and then, lest he forget The Plan, and how well it had worked out for him. *And we wouldn't want that.*

Daddy had given her that little piece of advice the night before their wedding. He'd said, "Why Bunnykins, every now and then,

I have to remind your mother where she was when I first met her and where she'd still be if I hadn't rescued her from endless cans of Chef Boy-ar-Dee, and I advise you to do the same with young Daniel. It's surely worked like a charm all these years for me."

Well, thought Bunny, while she rinsed the bubblegum-scented shampoo from her hair, it certainly had kept June Senior in line, so to speak. Danny, on the other hand, was another bowl of jelly beans. For one thing, Danny was much better looking than June Senior had ever been. He was smarter, certainly more athletic, and of course, there was his smile.

All of Bunny's friends told her they thought Dan was a real catch, and she believed them. She could tell by the way they looked at him sometimes, and vice versa, that she'd done well for herself. *See, it wasn't easy keeping him in line, Daddy, not like it was for you with Mommy.* She stepped out of the shower and wrapped herself in a fluffy white towel, one with her name, "Bunny," embroidered in curly pink letters—and she wondered. She couldn't help herself. For some strange reason, That Woman from the club was on her mind.

"Thank you, Felicity," June said.

The small woman finished filling June's bone china coffee cup and turned to leave, struggling to balance the oversized silver coffee pot. The worry lines on her forehead looked more prominent this morning, bathed in the morning sunlight that streamed through the sheer curtains. June, however, did not notice them.

"You know, Giles," June Senior said, lifting her pointed chin, "you look different to me this morning. Did you know that?" She studied the plain cornflakes in the flowered bone china bowl in front of her, and sprinkled two generous spoonfuls of sugar over them. "These need some bananas or something, don't you think so, Giles? Giles, whatever is on your mind?"

"Mind?" replied her husband. "I don't mind. Whatever you think is best, darling." He took a sip from his cup. Meanwhile, his toast and marmalade remained untouched.

"Oh, Felicity!" June said. "Could you please bring me some sliced bananas?"

Giles nodded and snatched his silver spoon. "Of course, June. Bananas are too plain."

June frowned and stared at the cornflakes. Don't you just love cereal? You know, I like my food plain, but not too plain, don't you agree, Giles?"

"Yes, well." For a second, June seemed speechless, but the moment didn't last. "You know, I spoke to Bunny this morning."

Giles munched his toast. His mouth full of crumbs, marmalade dripping from his lips, he attempted an answer. "Bananas, June. Right."

"Well, I don't know if you've noticed it or not, but you know, Dan just seems so distracted these days, even when he's with Bunny. And cross! Did you hear the way he snapped at me the other day? Well, of course you did, what am I saying?"

Without a word, Felicity entered the dining room bearing a small dish of sliced bananas on a silver tray. Her narrow mouth pursed in restraint, she set the dish next to June, her eyes downcast.

"Thank you, Felicity," June said. She took a deep breath and arranged some banana slices on the cereal, then trickled some milk from a tiny bone china pitcher into the bowl. She paused until the maid had left the room to continue her interrogation. "So, tell me Giles, what do you think? You don't suspect anything foul, do you? But seriously now, Giles, don't you think that Dan is a bit distracted these days? You do think so, I can tell, I just know you agree with me on this."

She opened her mouth with the tiny yellow teeth, and took a large bite of soggy cornflakes and bananas. A fly landed on the back of Giles' hand. He whisked it off and rose from the table. His gaze seemed fixed on a distant object.

"Chicken will be fine, June. See you tonight, darling." He strolled through the door and down the drive and through the massive gates, where Rocco waited with the Mercedes. Time to check up on young Daniel.

June ate her cornflakes and bananas in silence. *What was that about a chicken? Hmmm, couldn't possibly say. Giles rambled on about so many things, didn't he?* Well, all right then, as Giles wished. She supposed they would have chicken tonight.

Leila ran her long fingers through her thick, dark hair and sighed. What a morning it had been already, and now, she would head back to her hotel room. She wanted some time to think. For one thing, that stranger at the Cinnabar Club loomed large in her imagination. Why he had caught her eye, well, she couldn't say exactly, but…there it stayed. The love bug had bitten. She had to know who he was. But, she asked herself, why? She didn't need another lover, did she? There was something about this one that magnetized her, though. Yes, it was his smile. Beautiful. Promising. Young. That was it, she decided. He made her feel young again, and she loved that feeling. She loved it very much.

Maybe the waiter at the Cinnabar would know his name; the one who resembled the man that had driven her to her first sitting this morning. She wondered if he worked at the club. Well, she thought, while digging in the depths of her sack-like purse for her cell phone, there was one way to find out.

She would not wait for long. Almost as soon as she found the phone, it rang.

"Leila Bolivar?" said a man's voice.

Leila frowned. She couldn't quite place it, but the voice sounded oddly familiar. Okay, she decided, she would answer. "Yes," was all she said.

"This is Rocco Suarez, your driver from this morning, ma'am."

Leila felt puzzled. How did he know that she was preparing to call a driver? Hmmm. "Yes, I remember." *Go on, I'm waiting.*

Rocco cleared his throat. "Yes, ma'am. I wondered if you would be dining at the Cinnabar Club again, perhaps sometime very soon, ma'am."

Hmmm. Yes, now she understood. Rocco worked as a waiter at the Cinnabar Club. That's when she first noticed him. Apparently, he had noticed her too. Was he asking her out?

"I'm not sure, Rocco. Why do you ask?"

"I have a friend, Miss Bolivar, who would very much like to meet you."

"A friend?"

"*Sí.*"

"You know, I was just getting ready to call a taxi, but if you could pick me up..."

"If I could, I would, believe me. But, I cannot leave the club, you know."

"Well, what did you have in mind? It's after one o'clock now."

"My friend is here with me now, Miss Bolivar. Would you like to speak with him?"

Leila felt intrigued, though she knew she should be discreet. Instinctively, she knew this. And so, she would wait.

"I think I will wait. I prefer to meet a person in person. It's so much more, personal, don't you agree?"

A pause lingered.

"Rocco, are you there?"

"Oh yes, Miss Bolivar. It's just that, my friend here, he says that you've already seen him. At the Cinnabar Club, in the dining room. He is sure—well, he is really certain—you would remember him."

Leila gasped. Could it be? Then she swallowed, hard. Could it be a trap? After all, she didn't know this Rocco well at all. One could say that she did know Giles Dingwerth though, and he certainly had strong connections to the Cinnabar and evidently, to Rocco too. No, she would not go to the Cinnabar Club to dine. It was too risky, at least for her tastes.

"I will meet your friend, Rocco, but, well...he will come to me. I am staying at the Hotel Charlotte on Romine Avenue. How does four o'clock sound, for a drink or two?"

Not five seconds later, Leila glowed with anticipation.

"Four o'clock, then. I'll be waiting."

Four

"Danny? Well, what do you want to know?" Bunny's nose crinkled in amusement. "You always ask about him, Penny." The blonde studied her auburn-haired friend and giggled. "I'm starting to think you have a thing for my new husband." She smacked her glossy lips and sipped from her frosty strawberry daiquiri, garnished with a tiny pink paper umbrella. This, she removed from the rim of the tall glass, and proceeded to open and close it while she spoke. "Look at this! It's hot pink. I just love pink, if it's really hot, don't you, Penny? Penny, what are you staring at?"

Penny leaned against the round patio table and straightened her white plastic sunglasses. "Tell me I'm crazy, Candy, but isn't that Bunny's Danny over there, jabbering away on his cell?"

Like Bunny, Candy was a blonde. Unlike Bunny—aka June—Candy was Candy's real name. Candy, however, had other unique attributes that were not real. Like, for example, her nose, and obviously her platinum hair, and um well, her blouse-busting breasts. She crossed and uncrossed her long tanned legs and squinted in the appointed direction.

"Absolutely. It's Danny Hunt-er. Just look at that smile. Wonder what he's up to?"

Bunny closed the mini-umbrella and laid it on the table. "What kind of remark is that?"

"Well," Penny said, "did you know he was coming here for lunch? I mean, I guess that's what he's up to."

"Well," Bunny said, her pink mouth poised in a pout, "I didn't tell him I was coming here for tennis today. It just didn't come up. That's all there is to it."

"Right," Candy said. "It's probably nothing. Just a coincidence. So, go on over and give him a great big old kiss, why don't you?"

"Or," Penny said, "you could wait until later tonight and just ask him, 'Say hon, where did you eat lunch today?'"

Bunny snatched the umbrella, twirling it while she pondered the predicament. A quick glance told her that her husband had departed—in a hurry, it seemed.

"'Kay, 'kay. That's exactly what I'll do." She grinned and sipped at her drink. Her tanned face wore a triumphant expression. "Thanks, guys."

Giles opened the door to his spacious office and flipped on the florescent lights. At first, he wondered why his secretary hadn't already done this, and then, he remembered that Melanie had the day off. Well, poor thing, she needed it, didn't she? Getting married again, for God's sake, what was this, her third husband?

Giles shook his head and plopped down in the leather chair behind his oversized mahogany desk. Much simpler, wasn't it, to do things his way. He and the Junebug had been married for 36 or was it 38—he could never get it straight—years now, and if he got restless every now and then, why, he took care of it. Not divorce, never divorce. Too expensive. There were other ways. Like Leila.

Leila. He reached for the phone, and then remembered. She said she'd call, didn't she? Well. Giles glanced at the clock. One thirty. Maybe he'd go down the hall and see about what his Vice-President in Charge of—now, what had he put young Daniel in charge of, he could never get it straight—well, it didn't matter, did it?

He rose from his chair and sauntered down the empty hall. Daniel needed a job, that was all there was to it. And, he'd given him one. He'd taken care of it. He had everything under control. Giles Dingwerth felt good.

Until…until he strode into Daniel's sunny, spacious, corner

office. Clearly, young Daniel hadn't been in charge of anything today. And, thought Giles, he was supposed to be in charge of something. Why, the engraved nameplate on his door said so: *Daniel Hunter, Vice-President.* Right? So, where was he?

It was then that his cell phone rang. The familiar tune, "When the Saints Come Marching In" told him so. Well, it had to be Leila. That would cheer him up. Now, he was thankful for the privacy of Daniel's office. He answered the phone.

"Hello?"

"Giles, it's Leila." She sounded rushed, even businesslike. So unlike her, really. Well, it didn't matter.

"Yes, darling. When can I see you again?"

"That's what I'm calling about. I may need to go out of town for the weekend."

"Oh? Did you know about this?" His wandering eye drifted to a framed portrait of his daughter's wedding day—the whole family—just sitting there on Daniel's desk.

"No. Well, I suspected it, Giles. You know how this business can be."

Giles cleared his throat. "Where are you going?"

"What is it, darling?"

"I said, where are you going?"

"I'm not quite sure yet, and Giles, I need to go now, I really do."

"I miss you terribly."

"What?"

"Nothing. When will you be back?"

"I should be back Sunday evening at the latest. You can call my hotel if you'd like."

Odd, thought Giles. Very odd. "Tell you what. Call me when you know where you're going. I'd just like to know."

"I'll try," he heard her say, just before she clicked off the line. Had he been unreasonable in wanting to know where his lover of six months was going for the weekend? He didn't think so. And yet...well, there was no obligation on her part, or his for that matter, to explain their whereabouts. It was the unspoken "rule" between them, was it not? One of his very own, in fact. He'd made that plain from the beginning.

Ah, he thought—stabbed by his own dagger.

Dan tiptoed into his "not so little" house. *Crazy.* Here he was, sneaking around in his own home, trying to change his own clothes, without telling his own wife. *Crazy.* The afternoon sun filtered through the gauzy bedroom curtains, casting shadows on the perfect walls. Those shadows made him feel guilty. Okay…so, he wouldn't look. After all, what Bunny didn't know couldn't hurt her—right? And, the fact of the matter was, there was a lot that Bunny didn't know. In fact, that was one of Dan's favorite things about her.

Now, he stood in his extra organized walk-in closet, evaluating his "casual options." How casual should he go? The lady had proposed drinks, not dinner, but what if drinks turned into dinner? Would they? For a moment, Dan was stunned. If they did, what would he tell Bunny?

He grabbed a red knit polo shirt and a pair of khaki twill trousers. He would worry about Bunny later. Nothing would stand in his way now. He would meet Leila. What would he say to her? How would the afternoon unfold, hmmm? Leila, Leila. He buttoned the bottom third button of the shirt and smiled. He liked that name. Sensuous, but not too sensuous. In any case, much better than Bunny.

He checked the time—almost three o'clock. For a fleeting moment, he wondered if he'd been missed at work today. Then, he decided. Number one, it was Friday, number two, it was Friday afternoon, and number three, he really didn't believe he could ever be fired. Well, he virtually knew it. So, he put that thought right out of his mind. Time to think about the Hotel Charlotte… and Leila.

"Daddy?"

"Yes, Bunnykins," Giles said.

Back in his own office, he reclined in his leather chair. His feet crossed at the ankles, they rested on the edge of the executive size desk. He'd been terribly busy pondering the whereabouts of Daniel, Leila's curious apathy, and of course, whatever he would do this weekend with Leila out of town, when his desk phone rang. Well, a phone call from Bunny always cheered him. Even if he suspected she wanted money—again—which she almost certainly did.

"How are you?"

A peal of giggles echoed from the receiver. "I'm fine, Daddy. I'm always fine, aren't I?"

"Yes, you are. How's Daniel feeling these days? Is he sick?"

"Sick? You're just like Mommy; when I talked to her earlier this morning, she wanted to know if Danny was feeling all right too. Why are you asking me the same thing?"

Giles swung his shiny shoes onto the thick carpet and rested his elbows on his desktop. "Well, he's not at work today, Bunns. I haven't heard from him, so…obviously, he must be sick, hmmm?"

"He's not sick, Daddy. I just saw him at the club talking on his cell."

"At the club? You mean, the Cinnabar?"

"Well, where else? It's the only place I can get court time on Friday, isn't it? You know that, Daddy."

"Poor Bunnykins. Have you tried other places?"

"Daddy! How could you ask such a thing?"

"Well, I was just wondering. Back to Daniel. You say you saw him at the club?"

"Yes, Daddy. Honestly, you just ask the silliest questions sometimes."

"Did you talk to him? Ask him why he wasn't laboring away for the three D's this afternoon?"

"No, Daddy." Bunny sounded bored. "I was sitting with Penny and Candy, and they suggested, well somebody did, that I ask him where he had lunch today. You know, see what he says. Kind of like a joke on him, you know?"

"Umm-mm," said Giles, shaking his head. He knew only too well about jokes like that. Only too well.

"Bye, Bunnykins," he said.

Squeaky kisses into the phone. "Bye, Daddy. Bye-bye."

Then it hit him. Bunny hadn't asked for money. She'd just called to say hello and goodbye, which is mostly what Bunny always had to say, along with a few other tidbits, and that was that. For a moment, he stared at the family wedding portrait on his desk. His gaze centered on Bunny and Daniel. Why, if that boy ever hurt Bunnykins, he'd kill him. He would.

Just the thought of such an infraction made his face as red as a tomato. Well…no need to get so excited. Daniel probably had a very good reason for his unexplained absence this afternoon.

Personally, Giles couldn't wait to hear it.

Dan circled the block several times, trying to decide where to park his Porsche. It had been a tough decision to bring it, rather than call a taxi. If he left it behind, especially at home, he might have to explain why he left it behind, whereas if he drove it himself, he had to find an inconspicuous—like, invisible—place to park it. Like now. His whole problem, he decided, stemmed from inexperience. He was a novice at this game. From her specific instructions, he had gotten the definite impression that Leila Bolivar was not. A raspy voice startled him.

"Hey! You loss' or somethin'?"

Dan found himself idling in front of the Hotel Charlotte, staring into the curious, yet knowing eyes of a black man somewhere in his sixties. A grizzled gray stubble covered his chin. His green work shirt bore the name "Luther" embroidered in red thread.

"It's jus' that I done watched you go roun' the block three times now like you lookin' for somethin' you cain't fine. Maybe I can help you, man."

Dan glimpsed the time on the bank clock across the street. Three forty-five. "I need to park my car is all. I have an appointment at four."

Luther grinned. "Well hey, why didn't you say so? That's my job. Jus' gimme the keys. Where's your 'pointment?"

"Uh listen, I can just park it myself. Is there a garage nearby?"

"What's your problem? Naw, there's never been a garage exacly—gettin' fancy on me here—it's jus' Luther's Fine Parking, is what I like to call it. Which is jus' a fancy name for 'You Park It, I Watch It,' all for the bargain price of twenty-two dollars a day or four an hour, whichever you prefer. By the way, I accept tips. Where did you say your 'pointment was?"

The bank clock chimed four o'clock. Dan threw the keys at Luther. "Here, you park it and you watch it. I don't have time to do both." He pointed to the gold gilt building to his left. "This the Hotel Charlotte?"

"It be that," said Luther. "Listen, when you thinkin' you gone be back?"

Dan flashed The Smile. "Either six or who knows?"

Luther rolled his eyes and slid behind the wheel. "Whooeee! Take your time boy," was all he said.

Five

A light drizzle sprayed the sidewalk and Gabby Knowes, Society Gossip Columnist, darted for the revolving doors at the Hotel Charlotte. She was a tall young woman, about 5'10", with a mane of tangled copper hair and long scarlet fingernails. Light powder coated her porcelain skin, and square tortoiseshell framed sunglasses shaded her blue eyes. In a feverish haste, a young man dashed into the whirling glass cyclone beside her. She stumbled, and dropped a box of fresh glazed donuts onto the wet, greasy floor. The soft, crusty pieces flattened and ripped while the glass doors swirled and twirled. The normal flow of traffic slowed.

"Hey, you big jerk! Come back here!" Gabby said. For a moment, she thought Tom Cruise had nudged her. Why hadn't he helped her clean up the doughy mess? In fact, the young man rushed into the waiting elevator. Apparently, he believed the crowd wouldn't notice him. To the contrary, his hasty retreat only insured that they did. Where had she seen that guy?

Like lightning, it struck her. Dingwerth Distinctive Designs, that's where. The day she'd tried to interview that pompous patriarch for a feature article in the Gateway Gabette—yeah, that younger guy was his Vice-President in Charge of Something. She couldn't remember what. Come to think of it, she'd brought a box of donuts with her that day too. That day, no one had knocked her over, but she hadn't gotten the interview either. Well, she'd just make another appointment to get back into, what had the old goat called it, the Three D's? Not for nothing did people call her The Hurricane.

Now, the redhead approached the Front Desk. Surely, they would call Security! But, Security, all two guards of it, was engaged in rescuing a toddler from a stalled elevator. The desk clerk studied her for a moment and mumbled that she certainly didn't look "stalled" to him. The nerve! If she had anything to say about it—and she always did—she'd splatter the front page of the Gateway Gabette with that careless remark. She would.

Gabby stared while the housekeeping staff struggled to clean up the soggy bits from the sugar-glazed foyer. Her blue eyes observed each and every detail. While she watched the sweeping, the spraying, the mopping, her thoughts churned.

In the meantime…

She tramped back over to the marble topped front desk and dinged the brass bell. A young man with wavy brown hair stared back at her. "Madam?" he said.

The redhead whipped a business card from her red envelope-style clutch purse. She leaned in towards the man and whispered, "Look, you know that donut mess back there? Well, here's my card. If you hear anything, I mean anything, about the people involved, anything, please, please give me a call. There could be a little cash in it for you if you know what I mean. My name's right on there, see? It's Gabby. Gabby Knowes."

She turned and stomped into the lobby. Where to now? She checked her watch. She felt like a bourbon and water. If she hurried, she could catch happy hour in the hotel lounge.

She hurried.

Dan couldn't believe his luck. He guessed that's what he would call it. Actually, he didn't know what to call it, because he'd never experienced anything like it—the thrill, the surge, the drive that consumed him like a blazing fever. He craved more of it, whatever it was. He craved more, and he craved all of it.

Her long fingers entwined the crystal tumbler, the tips tracing little circles into the droplets. It was only a matter of time, this, they both knew. They couldn't explain the feeling that they'd both been here before, but they knew that couldn't have been. That they'd known each other for years, maybe forever, but they both knew that they hadn't. And, that they were destined to be together forever, but, ah forever, well…they had both already pledged that eternity to someone else.

They had this moment. This, they knew. Absolutely.

"So," said Leila, her lush red lips curling at the ends, "it's Dan, is it? Dan Hunter. I like that name." She tossed her head and her long, raven hair tumbled down the arch of her back. "You know who I am. You know, I wanted you from the moment I saw you. Did you know that?" She squeezed his hand.

Dan thought he would melt. What was happening to him? He sipped at his Scotch and water. Something gnawed at his brain, and even his gut. What was it? He smiled The Smile. He gazed into her dark eyes. "There's still something I don't know that I would very much like to know more about—if you don't mind."

"Yes?" Her eyebrows arched in mock wonder. Again, her lips curled at the ends. "What is that?" She sipped at her drink, a rum and Coke.

"How did we, uh, connect today?"

Leila batted her thick black lashes. "I don't know what you mean. You are a friend of Rocco's, aren't you?"

"Yes. Well, yes, that's right." That still didn't tell him how Rocco got his information, but if he wasn't careful, he could see now that he was going to ruin the moment. After all, what did it matter anyway?

Leila smiled. "That's what I thought." She drained her glass.

"Another?" Dan said.

"No," Leila said, "I prefer to go to my room."

"Oh."

She slid the room key across the table. Her eyes locked with his in a solitary stare. "Dan," she said in a low voice, "get the check."

Gabby had just ordered some bourbon on the rocks when she saw them. She spotted Dan at once, and of course, she knew Leila Bolivar. Who didn't? In fact, and this was crazy, she'd even heard those wild rumors about that rich Dingwerth Designs guy and her having an affair, but come on now, what would she want with Giles Dingwerth? Until now, Gabby never cared enough to delve into the murky details, but now—oh, here was the waiter with her drink—now, she might do just that. She watched Dan and Leila disappear into the paneled hotel lobby. Looked to her like there was a juicy story there.

She yanked a ten-dollar bill from her wallet and laid it on the table next to her still brimming tumbler. She had to leave. Now. The crowd milled around the lounge, impeding her hot pursuit of that slimy jerk. After the mess he'd made, she couldn't believe he hadn't left the hotel, but a woman like Leila Bolivar could make a man forget his own name, or so Gabby been told…

She watched them as they strolled together into the waiting elevator, lost in the cocoon of their private Nirvana, oblivious to prying eyes. Vibes electrified the air; Gabby could feel the tension between them. The elevator doors closed, and there she stood, all alone. How could she get that guy's name? She would have to be creative. Well, it wouldn't be the first time. And, she'd be willing to bet, he'd be upstairs for awhile this evening.

"Mommy?"

"Yes, Bunny." June Senior sat at her usual place at the massive dining room table, directly across from Giles, at the distant opposite end. As she had requested, Felicity had delivered the telephone on an ornate silver tray, and now, June turned to her husband in alarm.

"Giles, it's Bunny."

Giles stared at his gold-rimmed dinner plate and frowned. "I thought you said we were having chicken tonight, June."

June pursed her thin lips in exasperation.

"We are. I mean, it is."

"It's what?"

"It's chicken, Giles."

"I thought you said it was bunny."

"For heaven sakes, Giles, I'm talking to Bunny on the telephone. Now, eat your chicken."

Felicity stifled a giggle. The ponderous tray rattled on her outstretched palm. June swirled the gray-brown gravy into her mashed potatoes with the tines of her silver fork.

"Well, didn't he call? Nothing at all? For heaven sakes, have you tried to call him?"

She shoveled a forkful of beige-brown potatoes into her narrow mouth. "Odd. Very odd."

Giles stabbed a crisp green snow pea with his fork. He sat with his hand poised in midair, gesturing with the loaded fork while he talked. "June, can't this wait until we're finished eating? Why isn't Bunny eating?"

"Because Dan is missing."

Giles munched his snow pea. He swallowed before he spoke. "He isn't missing. He can't be missing. He's Vice-President in Charge of Something, don't ask me what. But I do know he is not missing. Bunny just doesn't know where to look, that's all. Did she try to call him on his cell?"

"Of course, Giles. But missing persons don't answer the phone."

"What time is it?"

"It is seven-thirty, sir," Felicity said. "Will you be having coffee this evening?"

"Yes, Felicity, we will," Giles said. "June, tell Bunnykins—well here, hand me the blasted phone. Bunns? Stop crying, Bunns. I'm sure he's fine. Well no, I didn't see Daniel this afternoon, but I don't always. You know how Fridays are. How are they? Well, they're loose honey, they're casual, they're—"

"Giles, you're not helping," June Senior said. "Now, give me that phone."

Felicity recognized that certain steel in Mrs. Dingwerth's

voice, that stuff reserved for the very special of special occasions. Oooh, she thought, her spindly arms aching to rest the silver tray on the polished cherry sideboard, a "special occasion" had arrived. *Oooh la la.*

"Now Bunny, you listen to me," June said. "I don't care what Daddy says. Daddy will find Dan for you. Of course he can. Daddy can do anything when Daddy decides to, isn't that right, Giles? Giles, I said *Giles*, isn't that right?"

Mr. Dingwerth nodded in submission. Felicity recalled another time she had seen that happen in her seventeen year employment with the Dingwerth household—the time Mrs. Dingwerth had decided Bunny needed a perfect larger house to go with her perfect larger diamond engagement ring. Well, Miss Bunny got the house and the diamond. She even got Dan Hunter for a while. Now, Mr. Dingwerth would find him and get him back, because Mrs. Dingwerth always got what she wanted. Of this, Felicity was certain.

She watched Mrs. Dingwerth place the telephone on the silver tray. Her petite frame flinched under the pressure. The tension in the room electrified, and Felicity embraced a reason to depart. Coffee. She would make the coffee. Tonight, the coffee would need some extra preparation time, to allow the Dingwerths some of their own. This, she would personally guarantee.

The door barely closed when Dan felt her arms encircle his waist. Her lips were on his, and he gasped. Somehow, he'd expected more banter, more booze, more time, but Leila didn't waste one precious second. She seemed like a ravenous tigress, hunting for food. Somewhere in the recesses of his mind, the word echoed, resounded, and repeated. *Food, food, food.*

He'd never intended to cheat on Bunny. Had he? No, he assured himself, even as Leila slid her long, tender fingers under his red knit polo shirt, gripping the flesh of his back between her scarlet nails. Really, he had expected a little preliminary conversation before…

Before what? What was he saying? He'd expected to keep

cool control no matter what. What a fool he'd been! Well, now, he reasoned, calm down a second. He hadn't lost control of the situation yet; he could get it back anytime he wanted, and really, he hadn't done anything to be that ashamed of—yet.

How the next two hours passed so quickly, Dan would never know. All he would ever remember for the rest of his life was the surreal euphoria, the driving sex that consumed him like a white hot heat, the wild hunger that fueled a fierce desire for more, more and still, more. He'd never experienced anyone-or anything-like Leila Bolivar. The more control he surrendered, the better he felt. Most of all, he liked who Leila made him—a man—not Bunny's Dan, or Mr. Dingwerth's slave. With her, he felt a virile identity that no one could reclaim. It was his to savor.

He sat up in the king-sized bed and checked his watch. 8:09. Leila lay beside him, bare-breasted, her cheeks flushed. She appeared to be asleep. Through the filmy sheer curtains, he studied the starless navy sky. He needed to get moving, he really did. It wouldn't be long, he just knew it, before Bunny, or worse, June Senior, began searching for him. In fact, he was astonished it hadn't happened yet.

He reached for his shirt, and she spoke. "Where are you going, darling?"

Darling. His body tingled at the sound of the words. "Leila, I need to…"

Brrring. The phone on the nightstand jingled. Dan's mouth twitched, the way it always did when he grew agitated—like now. The sinking feeling in the pit of his stomach told him he had been discovered. Leila would pick up that phone and the voice on the other end would be Bunny or June Senior, or even worse, Mr. Dingwerth.

Leila had actually been talking for a minute or so before he realized none of the formidable suspects were on the line. Even so, the sudden scare made relaxation impossible. Who was the caller?

"You shouldn't call so late, Carlos," Leila said. "Well, it is late here, and besides, I was asleep. Asleep. That's right, asleep for a change. Well, aren't you the fine one to talk, you with your little brats running around. No, you're right. Let's not mention your mistress. Carlos! I've had enough of this. I'm going to bed." She slammed down the receiver and stared at Dan. Her dark eyes flashed with fury. "And you, you're leaving." She gestured toward the door. "Go on, you've had your fun."

"Leila, I don't want to leave. It's just that Bunny..." Leila lit a cigarette and took a quick puff, blowing the smoke into the air in front of her.

"What bunny?"

"Bunny, my wife, she..."

"You're married to a rabbit?" Leila's voice exploded into ripples of laughter.

"No. Bunny is her nickname. Leila, please. Try to understand. I never meant for things to move so fast between us, if you know what I mean."

Leila sucked another drag from her cigarette. "No, I don't know what you mean. You mean that you're sorry about us?"

"No—no, I never meant that. I..."

"You mean you don't want to see me again? Is that it?"

"No." This wasn't going well at all. "It's just that, well, you're married, right? It's just that I feel confused about all of this. Everything happened so fast. Don't get me wrong. I'm not sorry about anything, and I absolutely want to see you again. I guess I just wasn't ready for what happened."

Slowly, the corners of Leila's mouth turned up. She smiled. "Oh, you were ready for it. No mistake about that." She patted the empty spot on the bed beside her. "Come back to bed, darling."

"Well, Giles," June Senior said, "what are you going to do? You can't just sit there, not while Bunny's in tears. Felicity, where are those dessert mints?"

"Now June, you know you shouldn't have those," Giles said. "Remember your diabetes."

"I don't need to." She pecked the pink mints from the jumbled maze of pastel discs. "You seem to do a splendid job all by your-self. Besides, my doctor says my understanding of diabetes and my superb control of my condition is iron-clad. 'Iron-clad'. Those were his exact words to me. Why, I can practically forget all about it, is what he said. Which is what I absolutely intend to do."

Giles rose from the table. "Well, suit yourself, June. You usually do."

"Where are you going?" June popped a green mint into her narrow mouth, and chewed it with her tiny, yellow teeth.

"I'm going to call Daniel."

"Why do you have to leave to do that? Certainly you can make calls from right where you are."

"No, June, I can't."

"I don't understand."

June pecked the mints with her bright geranium tinted talons. They almost sounded like a dish of marbles clacking together when they moved. "What? Why aren't there more pink mints in this bowl? You know, they never put enough of the really good things in a mix like this, did you ever notice that, Giles? Let me tell you, the pink ones are the best, and they try to make up for skimping by putting lots of green and yellow ones in, but they simply cannot make me happy that way. You can't substitute lots of something you don't want for a little bit of the one thing you do want, isn't that right?"

Her husband nodded. For once, he thought that maybe June was onto something. Now, he was thinking of Leila Bolivar. The one thing he really wanted, especially at this irritating, claustro-phobic moment. "I really must go. Bunns must be simply terri-fied, and a father can't allow that, not even for a moment. Stay right here, where I know I can reach you if I need to. You never know what I might find when I start asking questions."

June didn't hear a word he said. Actually, even as she picked through the multi-colored mints, she wasn't feeling quite well, no, she wasn't. Giles knew by the dazed look in her watery eyes that the candy had not agreed with her "condition." Well, he'd told her so himself, hadn't he?

It seemed like the perfect time to make his phone call—or calls, that is. He would do that right now.

"No, don't leave!" Leila said. "It's already late, Dan. Can't you just call her and say your car broke down, or I don't know, you got sick, or..."

"That I met someone?" Dan smiled. It was a sad, bittersweet grin. "How about the truth-that I've met someone unforgettable? Tell me, is that what I should say? By the way, I guess I don't really have the right to ask, but who is Carlos—is he your husband?"

Again, the shrill *brrring* of the phone.

"Always the phone," Leila said. "*Sí*, Carlos is my husband, who calls me all hours of the day and night." She yanked the receiver from its cradle. "Carlos! What is it?" Her voice lowered. She turned away from Dan.

For a moment, he even thought he saw the color drain from her face. Bad news from home? Had someone died? He felt somewhat guilty, eavesdropping like this, yet, Leila suddenly sounded so somber.

"No Giles, I can't see you now," she said. "Meet you? I have to get up early in the morning. Don't be crazy. It's only been a little while. You, come here? Now?"

A quick glance over her shoulder at Dan, who was already tying his shoe. "Giles," he'd heard her say. It couldn't be, could it?

"Oh, alright, then. For a nightcap. See you soon."

She turned to Dan. He stood and faced her, wondering how this could be, if it could be; if it could be, and it really could, should he ask? Yes, he decided, he should. He did. He tried not to flinch when he heard "Dingwerth." No recognition in his voice or on his face, he was confident of that. But, on his way to the car, after Leila swore her absolute discretion, he wondered something else.

How much did Rocco know?

Six

Gabby waited downstairs in the lobby for hours. She'd even had dinner with that desk clerk, Marc Stephens. Marc had needed someone to talk to, now that he and his partner, Brock, were considering a separation; and, Gabby was more than anxious to listen. He and Brock had tried couples counseling, but sometimes, he told Gabby in a confidential tone, he just didn't feel Brock was being totally honest. Gabby stabbed some leaves of fresh spinach with her fork and bit into the crispy greens, chewing in rapt attention. Now, Marc confessed that he was afraid that his worst fears had been realized.

Gabby's eyes grew wide with intrigue. "Tell me."

Marc's eyes grew teary. "Gabby, don't tell a soul..."

"You know I won't." She chewed slowly, her gaze never leaving his face. Finally, she swallowed.

"Oh, I know, but you know." He pulled a handkerchief from his coat pocket and wiped his eye. "People just don't understand. I mean, I feel so alone. I hate to burden you. You must think I'm an awful bore."

"Oh no, I don't. When you get boring, I'll tell you, how's that?"

Marc stared at his shrimp cocktail, almost as if he thought it might provide some answers. "Oh all right, you've convinced me." He snared a lemon wedge with his cocktail fork. "I guess our story isn't all that unusual."

"Tell me."

Marc dipped the jumbo piece of shrimp into some tangy

red cocktail sauce. He bit the end and closed his eyes. "A slice of heaven. Let me start at the beginning. I knew Brock was the one for me when he walked into the costume party last Halloween. I mean, I couldn't see his face at first, but there I was, all decked out in my wicked little nurse uniform, and here comes Brock with a stethoscope around his neck!" Marc blushed. "He was wearing a nurse costume, too. Now tell me, Gabby, what were the chances?"

"Of what?"

"Of both of us wanting to be a nurse for Halloween?" Gabby shook her head.

"I wouldn't even try to guess. But tell me, what went wrong? Marc, what is it?"

"I need more than five." Now Gabby felt confused and insanely curious. Should she ask?

"Five what?"

"Shrimp. I mean, would you take a look at this? Eleven ninety-five for five shrimp. Big ones, but still…well, back to your question." Again, a tear formed in the corner of his eye. "I just can't believe it's over. I mean, what did she have that I didn't?"

"Who?"

"Angela. Angela Hart."

"The doctor's wife?" Gabby doubted she could keep this a secret for long. Angela Hart had acquired quite a few new enemies since her divorce, well-known people who wouldn't mind trading secrets with Gabby Knowes.

"I can't believe it, Gabby. I never thought Brock would leave me for a woman, especially one like Angela Hart. It's just so, I don't know, so *not* him." He emptied two packets of Sweet 'n Low into his iced tea and stirred, shaking his head. "There's simply something wrong with the picture. She's not his type. She's short, she's plump, and she's way over forty. That is definitely not Brock Edwards let me tell you. But, and this is what I think it really is, Angela Hart is loaded! That's what she's got that I haven't—cash, and lots of it. Well, it's time to get back to the old salt mines. Gabby, what's wrong? Oh, I have bored you, haven't I?"

"It's not you," she said. "There's somebody I have to catch up with."

Marc watched her struggle through the revolving doors after the same guy that ruined her donuts. He guessed she wanted him to buy her another box. After all, what else would the nosiest gossip columnist in town want with a guy like that? Besides, thought Marc, if Gabby really wanted gossip, his story was much better. He was sure of that.

Luther was closing up for the night when he saw him. What a sight he was, too: rumpled shirt open at the collar, suit coat flapping in the wind, desperation written all over his dumb white face. That was the thing, man. This guy, whoever he was, whatever he'd just been going, whatever he was about to do, was desperate. Luther knew one thing about desperate people, and he was afraid of them, because…because, there was just no telling what they would do. That was the thing, man.

Looked to Luther like this guy might be wanting his fine car back. Well, well. He'd had him figured for the overnight parking. Guess things didn't work out, after all. Well, well. Luther sure knew how that tune sounded. Heads up. Here he comes now.

"Yes, sir," Luther said. "Parking or driving tonight? What will it be?"

"First of all, it's Dan, okay? Just call me Dan, everybody else does." He was fishing in his back pocket for his wallet. "How much for tonight, Luther?"

"Are you finding that Porsche or am I? Because I'm all alone tonight. Can't leave the entrance unattended, if you know what I mean. Get some mighty suspicious customers every now and then."

Dan nodded. "Yeah, okay. I understand. I'll get it myself."

"Forty will do then. I charge extra for the Porsche because I take extra care of it."

"I'm being ripped off, but what the hell, it's tonight's theme song." Dan peeled off two twenty-dollar bills and laid them in Luther's outstretched palm.

Luther shook his head and chuckled. "Ain't even going to ask why you said that...Dan, is it?"

"Don't. Just don't." Dan turned and took a few steps before turning to face him. "Listen Luther, uh, you didn't see me here tonight, did you?" He winked.

Luther stared at the two twenties in his palm. "Let's see now. Did I or didn't I?"

"Man!" Dan retraced his steps. "Okay, you got me." Another twenty-dollar bill changed hands. "Now, let's do this again. Was there anyone like me driving a black Porsche in here tonight?"

Luther grinned. "Not tonight, not last night, or maybe even tomorrow." He opened his palm once more. "How about next week?"

"Forget it," Dan said. "I could be dead next week."

Luther watched him walk away and he had to admit, he hadn't thought of that. He didn't have time to do much thinking. The wheels of the oncoming Mercedes crunched onto the gravel. He took a deep breath and jumped away from the curb. Guy could get killed just standing here minding his own business. Didn't even have to be working, which by the way, he was. The back passenger window slid down, and a white-haired head popped out.

"You! Seen a black Porsche tonight?"

Now this was too much, thought Luther; and to think he almost closed up for the night.

"Naw," he said scratching his head. "Not tonight, or last night, either."

"Sure about that?"

"Yeah."

He couldn't have known, but at that exact moment, Dan's black Porsche was leaving the garage exit directly behind him. He couldn't have known that Giles never saw the car or the driver, or that Rocco did see it, as well as the driver's face. No, he didn't know because Rocco didn't want him to know. At that moment, Rocco was wondering many things, but really he decided, just one thing mattered. None of these people could ever find out about the affairs of the others, or of his involvement, because if they did, Rocco was sure of one thing: next week, he could be, and most probably would be, dead.

Gabby watched the scene from the elevator doors. Of course, she recognized Giles Dingwerth, and of course she knew the jerk that ruined her donuts. Well, it was obvious to her: the Vice President in Charge of Something was leaving Leila Bolivar and—and, this was too delicious—Giles Dingwerth was going to meet her. Gabby would bet a box of Krispy Kremes—hot, fresh ones.

"Oh, Felicity?"

"Madam?"

Felicity hoped with all her heart that June Senior didn't want her to serve any more of those chalky pastel mints. She'd given her quite a scare not long ago. Not that they were anything new. At least once a week, June Senior called Dr. Hart, and he talked to her about her dietary indiscretions, which she'd usually deny outright. Like tonight.

"Oh no, Dr. Hart, I followed my diet like I follow my religion," she said with decided conviction.

Some religion, thought Felicity. So what did June Senior want now?

"Felicity, what time is it? I can't see that blasted clock without my glasses and Giles put them up before he left tonight."

"It is almost ten forty-five, madam. Would you like the television? Some chicken bullion?"

"No, nothing." June Senior sighed. "I've been thinking, though."

Uh-oh.

"Did I ever tell you about how I was when Giles met me?"

"How you were? What do you mean?"

"I mean, how I was. How things were for me. I wasn't always so well off, you know. Or maybe you didn't."

"Well, I didn't, madam, but forgive me, does it matter now? Look at all of this. All you need to think about is how nice your life is today, and tomorrow, and the next day. Correcto?"

"Well now, that's what I was going to tell you about. I do need to think about it, because Dan reminds me so much of myself, you know."

Stunned, Felicity stopped plumping the mounds of pillows. Up to this moment, she had firmly believed that June Senior despised Daniel Hunter, or at least, held him in utter disdain. But now…this revelation was simply unbelievable. She braced herself for what she knew was coming, like a sandcastle about to be razed by an incoming wave.

June Senior nestled in the pastel satin pillows. Her face was sallow and the skin around her jaw line sagged and drooped like melting wax. Absent scarlet lipstick, her thin lips were barely visible. She gazed off into the distance as she spoke. "You know, I don't believe I've really ever told anyone else this story…not even Bunny, come to think of it. Can you get me some wine?"

She began to cough, and Felicity hustled into the dim kitchen. June Senior was not well tonight. Even when she poured the red wine into the goblet and set it on the silver tray with a paper napkin, Felicity had a very uneasy feeling. She could only hope Mr. Dingwerth would return soon. When she entered the spacious master bedroom, she gasped.

June Senior had vomited on the front of her flannel nightgown, and was audibly choking. Felicity set down the tray and ran to her side. "Should I call Dr. Hart again?" she said, her voice quivering with panic.

"Giles," June Senior said, between labored breaths. "Call Giles."

Seven

Dan couldn't believe how quickly the time had passed. He cruised on the highway, amazed at the amount of traffic that surrounded him. On a typical night, he returned home by 11:00, snuggled next to Bunny.

He blinked hard, and struggled to keep his heavy eyelids from sagging. Until this moment, he hadn't realized how weary he felt. The day had been one big blur, from the time he left work to the time he finally retrieved his car from Luther's Fine Parking.

A relentless obsession with Leila Bolivar consumed his thoughts. Stolen moments with the love of his life were all that mattered now. Dan realized the risks. The stakes were high; but, he didn't care. Lady Luck was on his side. Restless, he flipped on the radio, and then, silenced it.

What bothered him so much? He had the world by the tail. All he had to do for the rest of his pathetic life was to tolerate Bunny's every whim. What was so hard about that? Ha! Just like Giles Dingwerth? After tonight, he didn't know what to think about his father-in-law. He punched the dashboard in frustration.

A fine mist coated the windshield and he turned on the wipers. A passing truck flung grimy muck onto the windshield of his Porsche, just before it passed him, just before he stomped the brakes, just before he rolled into the ditch beside the shoulder of the highway. It was the last thing Dan would remember about his luscious night.

It was almost midnight.

Had he really seen a black Porsche just a minute ago? Giles couldn't be sure, but as agitated as he felt at this moment, riding in the elevator up to Leila's room on the twelfth floor of the Hotel Charlotte, he simply erased the thought from his mind. That way, he had more room for his sole obsession, Leila Bolivar.

There were times, he had to admit, that he felt conflicted about his dalliance, but, he always reminded himself, what he had with Leila came once in a lifetime, if one was extremely lucky. Had he ever felt that way about June? If he had, he couldn't remember it.

The elevator door opened and Giles stepped out onto the padded carpet, navy covered in golden fleur de lis. No, he decided, he had not. At one time, when they were both young and naïve, perhaps he thought he had found true love with June. But, June would never be Leila.

Ah, Leila! He stopped in front of Room 1204 and cleared his throat, then smoothed his graying hair. He hoped he looked smashing. Leila always looked smashing. He knocked on the door and waited. At moments like these, his focus was intense, his adrenaline pulsing.

The door opened, and Giles felt beguiled. A second later, he was bewildered. What a time for his damn cell phone to ring! Certainly, he'd turned it off for the evening. How could he have been so distracted? His arm encircled Leila's narrow waist while he talked. A quizzical look lingered in her dark eyes.

"Yes Felicity, what is it?" he said, his voice peppered with a choppy impatience. "You know I'm out looking for Daniel." Was it his imagination, or had he felt Leila's body twitch just ever so slightly? "June? What's the matter with her now? Well, put her on then. What do you mean, you can't? If she just vomited…well then, let her sleep. No use calling Dr. Hart. He knows she breaks her diet left and right, with all those mashed potatoes and those tacky mints. You know, Felicity, you really ought to hide them. I do hope she didn't want anything to drink on top of it all. Wine? Oh, for the love of Pete. I'll be home as soon as possible. No, I don't know when that will be. Now please, let me find whatever it is I'm looking for. Good evening."

Leila tossed her head and laughed, a hoarse, throaty laugh. "Whatever it is you're looking for? And what is that?" she said in a mocking tone. She twisted a lock of her long hair around her forefinger. "Who is Daniel?"

Giles nuzzled her neck. Why on earth, now that they were finally alone for such a short sweet time, did Leila want to know about Daniel? His lips grazed hers and his eyes drifted to the king-sized bed. The sheets, uh, were quite rumpled, and say there, the pillows on both sides of the bed were quite mussed up. *Had Leila had company?*

"Darling." He pulled her closer to his chest. "Have you been quite alone this evening?"

Leila's face remained stoic, even as her wandering hands caressed the length of his firm body, finally lingering just below his waist. Craving her as he did, her touch felt like food to a starving man; like a drug for a desperate addict. He lived for these rationed interludes. Without them, he would die; of that, he felt certain. Only these times could sustain him through the mindless exchanges with June, and the endless parade of social engagements arranged by her or her meddlesome cronies. As long as he had Leila in his life, he could survive.

Her fingers undid his tailored trousers and they fell to the floor around his ankles. She dropped to her knees in front of him. In an instant, Giles knew one thing. They would not need the bed tonight.

"So, uh, Rocky, did you say your name was?" Luther asked. He pulled a half empty pint of whiskey from behind a pile of boxes. "How about a little drink or three?"

They sat side by side in the tiny one room building that served as Luther's main office. It had one desk, one ancient, or "antique" as Luther liked to call it, brass lamp, a short row of rusty file cabinets, and a wall covered in scraped, brown pegboard that held rows and rows of keys. Rocco found himself gawking at them in amazement. How did Luther keep them all straight? He asked him that now, but Luther seemed too preoccupied with refreshments to hear him.

The old man leaned back in his squeaky desk chair and sighed. Then, he took a long swig from his amber root beer bottle, just before he set out two paper cups leftover from last year's Christmas party at his tidy home on St. Martin Avenue. "Hey Rocky, you like the Santa Claus on your cup, or how 'bout a reindeer?" he said, filling both cups half full with liquor.

"Really, I should not drink and drive," Rocco said. "I would just like to know how you take care of so many fine cars. Very 'spensive, eh? How you remember what car belongs to who?"

"Eenie meanie minie moe." Luther pointed from one cup to the next. His calloused finger finally rested on the Santa Claus cup. "See, it's like this. I got a gift." He gulped from the cup. "Ah! Glad you stopped by, bro'."

"A gift, you say?"

"Yeah. Like, when somebody hands over their keys to they car, I see they face up in my brain. Got it? Keys in the hand, face in the head."

"So, how that help you?"

Luther slurped another gulp from the cup. "Well like, tonight for example. There was this guy, call me Dan, he tells me, all up in a hassle to get to a four o'clock 'pointment. He got hisself a fine black Porsche. Me being me, I take the keys, and I make a mental note of his face, you know, like I done told you about."

"Why?" Rocco said.

Luther drained the cup and reached for the other one.

"Why? Now how do I know? It's like my gift, man, I'm telling you, so listen up. Anyways, I got this guy Dan figured for my fine overnight parking, but lo and behold, what do you know? Here the man done cometh along 'bout ten, ten thirty to get his fine black car. Didn't mind babysitting that machine, nossir. But, let me tell you brother, I knew him in an instant, and I knew he belonged to the black Porsche. Didn't keep me from charging him forty dollars for the extra fine care I gave it neither. But see? That's what I'm talking 'bout. I got a gift. You get me now, Rocky?"

"This Dan, uh, what he look like, amigo?"

"Well now, I shouldn't pass that on, 'cause of confidentiality and all, but hey, you know how to keep a secret, don't cha? Yeah, I thought so. For starters, he was white, real white. Kinda look like that movie star, you know, Tom Cruise, yeah. Got that big smile. Why, you think maybe you know somebody like him?"

Rocco shrugged. "Maybe."

"Well now, wouldn't that be some trip. Say, what are you doing here anyways?"

Before Rocco could answer, both men looked up to see Giles Dingwerth approaching the office. His face wore a contented smile.

"Looks like my time is up," Rocco said. "Nice to meet you."

Luther rose from his seat and yawned. "Yeah, me too. Maybe now I can get in a little shut eye. All this socializing done wore me out."

Rocco winked. "I got a feeling you're not the only one feeling that way tonight, amigo."

The rain pelted across the windshield of her car, and Gabby pulled her red BMW onto the shoulder of the highway to wait— wait until the storm subsided, at least a little, or a lot. It didn't matter now. After trailing the Porsche for a few miles, she was lost. Well, that idea was crazy anyway. After all, what did she think might happen? There was no reason for a guy to pull over, just because some zealous reporter wanted to interrogate him. No reason, except...

Gabby couldn't believe her break. Even in the driving rain, she could tell it was him, crashed in that ditch. Had someone called for help? Should she call 911? No, she decided, she should not. She would do this in the rational, step by step approach she knew she could summon, if she really wanted to. She would talk to him first. So, where was an umbrella when she needed one?

After the potent drinks she'd consumed, her head felt lighter than her body. Headlights from passing cars blinded her vision. She ventured into the freezing rainstorm, and stumbled into a deep puddle. Great. Again, she asked herself, what did she think was going to happen tonight? Had this guy already called for help, or would he be glad to see her?

The moment she spotted him, she knew the answer. A deep gash marred the center of his forehead. Dark blood trickled from the corner of his open mouth. She wanted to scream. But wait, for everyone's sake here, Gabby knew she needed to remain calm. *Pull yourself together.*

The car leaned precariously at an angle. She cracked the passenger door, and climbed into the stuffy space. Her hand grazed a thick piece of smooth leather. As if it possessed a pair of guilty eyes, the wallet stared at her. Of course, she inspected the contents, Gabby being Gabby, and besides, she should know who he was, right? *Hmmm, nice wallet, lots of cash.*

The guy moaned. She opened the wallet and the driver's license spoke for itself: Daniel John Hunter in living color, smiling that big, wide smile. This certainly looked like the same guy that caused the donut ruckus at the hotel a few hours ago. Hunter, Hunter…where had she seen that name? Could it be that same one that married Bunny Dingwerth last year? That wedding splashed all over the society page, which left no room for anyone else— *that* caused quite a stir, yesirree. Now this was news! Well, she'd keep the wallet until the police arrived.

She punched 911 into her cell phone. She had no trouble providing her whereabouts, Dan Hunter's identity, or in what condition she'd found him. That was the easy part. It was later, when she sat waiting in the front seat of her car watching the rain droplets patter against her windshield, that she realized something, something truly bothersome, at least to her.

Why was Daniel Hunter lying in his Porsche in a ditch in the pattering midnight rain?

Giles remained remarkably quiet on the ride home. In Rocco's opinion, the old boy did not seem like himself these days. An ardent fan of bawdy jokes and limericks, Giles usually repeated a half dozen at a time. Indeed, mindless banter seemed to ease his toxic tension before he faced yet another meal with June Senior.

Outside, the air felt frosty and moist, but not quite cold enough for a solid freeze. Still, Rocco flipped on the heater. The hum of the blower was the only sound. About twenty minutes passed before Rocco drove the Mercedes onto the circular drive in front of the palatial Dingwerth residence.

"That's odd," Giles finally said.

"Sir?"

"I only meant that it was odd, Rocco, that the house would be so dark. Felicity usually leaves on more lights than that, doesn't she?"

"I wouldn't know sir, but—it is very late."

"It is? How late is it?"

"Past midnight, sir."

Giles flung the car door aside and gasped. "Oh, no. Oh, no."

Something told Rocco to wait until Giles opened the massive front door. True, the dark house concerned him, almost as much as the impulsive detour to the Hotel Charlotte. But, Felicity's frenzied phone call alarmed him in an inexplicable fashion. Less than an hour ago, Felicity confided to him that, earlier that evening, she called Mr. Dingwerth about an emergency concerning Mrs. Dingwerth's condition. His lackadaisical reaction made her very nervous. What if, say, Mrs. Dingwerth went into a coma? One can only do so much, thought Rocco, though he didn't say this to Felicity. In fact, he couldn't recall what he had advised her to do. His thoughts were interrupted. Giles raced to the car as if his feet were on fire.

"Hurry, Rocco!" Giles' voice sounded hoarse and frightened. "Get me to Ivymount Medical Center. Fast!"

"Hospital? Why?" Rocco suspected he knew the reason only too well, but this was no time for speculation.

"Felicity left a note on the front door, which by the way, I've instructed her never to do. June went to Ivymount Medical Center, by ambulance." He buried his head in his trembling hands. "Oh God, how could I?"

"Could you what, sir?"

"Drive, Rocco. Just drive. Now please, no more talking."

Rocco stared straight ahead and just drove. If he concentrated, he could probably make Ivymount Medical Center in less than fifteen minutes. Mr. Dingwerth didn't need to worry. He had no intention of talking.

Gabby decided to wait with Dan. It was the least she could do, she reasoned. After all, she needed to justify what she knew she was going to do with her fresh "scoop." After all, she was, first and foremost, a reporter, and she had a job to do. Still, she liked to think she had a humane side to her persona. And so, she would wait; at least until his wife or some other interested party whom she would definitely be interested in, appeared on the scene. Where were the guy's, uh, friends?

A couple of seconds later, she wished she hadn't asked that question. Bunny appeared in all her glory, clad in a powder pink sweat suit. Fuzzy white pompoms adorned her hooded sweatshirt. She was wearing white plastic sunglasses, and her lips were slicked with white frosted lip-gloss.

One swift look at Gabby and her frosted mouth froze in a pout. "Who are you?" she said, whisking away the sunglasses. Gabby noticed the fury lurking in those lined emerald eyes. Without waiting for an answer, Bunny forged ahead with her interrogation. "Don't tell me," she raged, throwing her white Prada purse on a nearby chair, "you are the reason Danny didn't come home tonight." She took a step toward Gabby. "Am I right?"

Gabby grinned. This was going to be such a good story! "I don't believe we've met. And, before you say another word, you really should know who I am. Just so you don't make a big mistake."

"Mistake? It looks to me like you're the one who made the

big mistake. Who are you?"

"I am Gabrielle Knowes. You know, the Gateway Gabette? It's the local gossip column. Everybody who is anybody reads it. You may have heard of it—or not. Everybody calls me Gabby, so I guess you can, too, Bubbly."

"Who do you think you are, talking to me like that? Do you want to know who I am? I am Bunny Dingwerth Hunter. My father owns Dingwerth Distinctive Designs. And Danny works for him. He's Vice-President in charge of, of…um, Danny? Just look at him, all banged up like that. Well, he's in charge of something. Daddy knows what. So, don't try to impress me, Gumby."

"It's Gabby. By the way, I believe your father and I have already met."

"Well, stay away from my husband, whoever you are. We are very happily married." Bunny's eyes narrowed. "You know, I've suspected there was something going on for awhile now, so how do you like that? I know all about you now, so get lost. There's nothing more for us to talk about."

Gabby grabbed her purse and smoothed her rumpled clothes. *Well, she'd tried.* Even as she walked to her car, though, she grinned. She couldn't help herself. Bunny Dingwerth Hunter couldn't have been more wrong about her father, and her marriage and her Danny. *Rest assured, Bunny, there is so much more to talk about-and talking is what I do best.*

Eight

Beneath a blanket of twinkling stars, Dan slumped beside her. Gliding along the deserted highway, Bunny drove her white BMW, headed for her perfect larger house. Dan felt drowsy, to be sure. His temples throbbed. The real tension, however, pulsed between husband and wife. What, asked Bunny, did Danny have to say for himself, hmmm?

Dan really didn't want to have this conversation, not with Bunny...not now, not ever. For one thing, Bunny was just too shallow, too naïve, too *silly*, to ever begin to grasp what he felt when he was with Leila. He didn't even know if he could explain how he felt when Leila looked at him, or oh, when she touched him! One glance at Bunny, gazing straight ahead at the straight, dark stretch of road, white plastic sunglasses framing her eyes, and he absolutely knew one thing. He sure didn't understand his wife.

"Danny," she said with a chirp, "answer me. I know you're not asleep over there."

Dan tried to straighten his back. His body ached everywhere, in places he didn't know existed, until now. Okay, here goes. "Bunny, can't this thing wait?"

"No!" Her voice bordered on a screech. Her sneaker-clad feet jammed on the brake, and Dan's neck jerked. "Danny, I know all about her."

Dan felt a cold sweat on his clammy forehead. How in the...

"But Danny, it's not your fault."

Oh good. For a split second, Dan felt calm.

And then…

"Because I know how pushy women can be."

"You do?"

"Well yes. Sometimes, I'm paying attention." Again, she jammed on the brakes. The driver in back of her blared his horn in protest. Bunny giggled. "Ooops. Anyway, I took care of it and you don't ever have to worry about that woman bothering you again."

"What, uh…what did you do?"

"Why, I had a word with her. She knows who I am now, believe me. And do you know, she had the nerve to tell me she knew Daddy too?"

"She did? I mean…she does?"

"Yes. But, don't worry. She won't bother you anymore." The brakes squealed, and she peeled into the driveway of her perfect larger house. "Danny, I've been thinking." She removed her sunglasses and stared into his bloodshot eyes. "I want us to have a baby."

A thousand thoughts whirled through Dan's mind. In his groggy condition, he never thought to ask where Bunny had encountered the mysterious "her" that he no longer needed to fear. It never occurred to him that his wife could have been referring to anyone other than Leila. Leila was the only woman he ever thought about, anyway. Wait, what did Bunny say about a baby?

They couldn't have a baby! Leila was the woman he wanted to be with, not Bunny. Not Bunny and Bunny Baby. Now, he was so confused. This had not been his Plan. His head throbbed with fatigue, but he had to think-fast.

Looking back, he would suppose that this was the moment he decided to kill his wife. As she prattled on about her pregnant friends and her wannabe pregnant friends, Dan decided. It wasn't fair. Bunny didn't deserve to die. He wouldn't ever say that. But, it was the only way out, the only way to get, indeed, to keep, what he wanted. Nothing was going to stand in the way of his happiness with Leila Bolivar. Now, at last, he could sleep.

Once again, he had a Plan.

❖

"Where were you?" Felicity asked.

Rocco felt weary, especially of nosy questions. How much should he tell her? Or perhaps a better question would be, how much did she already know? The frazzled woman lingered in the drafty hospital corridor. The high ceilings and extra wide halls of Ivymount Medical Center dwarfed her petite stature and indeed, her significance. Would this night never end?

"I was looking for you—and trying to find out something about Mrs. Dingwerth—but, they wouldn't tell me anything besides her room number. Do you know anything?" A quick glance in the direction of Mrs. Dingwerth's hospital room told him she didn't want visitors. The white enameled door remained closed.

"Want to get some coffee?" she said.

Rocco nodded. "We have a few minutes, I guess. Mr. Dingwerth just got here. I saw a lounge at the end of the hall. Let's go."

Felicity looked relieved. "Okay. I could sure use a break, I'm telling you. My back is aching so bad you don't know. Mrs. Dingwerth fell, and I had to lift her by myself. I wasn't sure I could do it."

"She fell?" Rocco strolled briskly beside her.

"Sí. And, I could not wake her. That's when I called Mr. Dingwerth." She shook her head. "But, it was too bad. He wouldn't come. So, I ask you now, Rocco. Where were you? What I mean is, where did you take Mr. Dingwerth tonight?"

The lounge resembled a doctor's waiting room, with its collection of straight backed vinyl chairs and outdated magazines. A murky blend of Lysol and steamed food hung in the stale air. Felicity and Rocco stared at the coffee pot, filled with thick brown sludge that had been simmering for hours.

"None for me," was all Felicity could say.

"Me neither," Rocco said.

"You didn't answer my question. Where did you take him?"

Ah, the moment of truth. Or was it? His reluctance to speak

seemed to speak for itself.

Felicity laughed. "You too, eh? Did he ask you not to tell anyone? Of course he did. It's okay. I know who she is."

"You do?"

"*Sí*. Mr. Dingwerth has brought her to the house to that guest bedroom in the west wing."

"I thought that part of the house was closed off."

Felicity winked. "It is, except when it isn't."

"Oh. How long has he been doing this, eh?"

"Six months? Seven? I don't know. Tell me something. How did he meet her?"

"This, I know," Rocco snickered. "It was at the Cinnabar Club. She came one night to meet a man who never showed up. Mr. Dingwerth was a lucky man; or, should I say, *is* a lucky man."

Felicity studied the closed door and sighed. "Is he?"

Behind the white enameled door, amid the antiseptic smells, the sucking, draining tubes and the starched white sheets, cleverly stamped with "Ivymount" in faded black ink across the hem, Giles did not feel, um, lucky. As he sat clasping June's clammy blue-veined hand in his own bear-like grip, he realized one thing with absolute clarity. He would never quit seeing Leila Bolivar, because very simply, he couldn't. He craved her like he hungered for food and air to breathe. Whatever it took, whatever the cost, he would bear it. He was her captive slave.

"So, Giles, is it?" Dr. Hart saidasked peering over his half glasses. "Haven't seen you in quite awhile. Been playing a lot of golf, have you?" The chubby man chortled at his own joke.

Giles did not appear to be amused. "No doctor, I have not been playing a lot of golf. My work is my obsession."

"Really?" The doctor set his clipboard on a chipped windowsill, and removed his glasses. "You know, that's not what your wife tells me."

Giles could feel his face flush a bright red. Well, there was nothing he could do about it. "What are you implying?"

"I am implying nothing. I'm going to be quite straight with

you. Your wife suspects you have a mistress."

"How dare you!"

"I am simply doing my job. Besides, you should know what your wife's thoughts are, don't you agree? It is also my duty to inform you that June is not well at all."

"Exactly what are you saying?"

"I am saying, she can't keep repeating these dastardly dietary indiscretions, she must take her medications on time, and she must reduce her stress levels. Or you, my friend, are not going to have a wife much longer. Tell me, does that grave possibility concern you?"

"Are you finished?"

Dr. Hart snatched his clipboard and glanced at the dozing patient. "Yes, I'm afraid I am." He shook his head. "Women. Studies in contradiction, I'm afraid. There's no understanding them." He was almost out the door when Giles stopped him.

"Doctor?"

A quizzical look answered his question. "You said something back there that quite bothered me. It was something about, well, about a mistress."

Dr. Hart's mouth turned up at the corners. "I think we both know what that is."

Giles' shoulders slumped in submission. To agree would have been suicide. He could see that. "Yes," was all he said. "Thank you for seeing June."

"You're welcome, Mr. Dingwerth," Dr. Hart said. "Please, for everyone's sake, be careful."

With a bang, the white enameled door slammed. Giles turned to focus on June. Beneath the harsh florescent lights, her thin skin ravaged by advanced age and poor health, he found it impossible to recall how she had once looked when she was young; that is, until he remembered Bunny. Bunny! He had forgotten to call Bunny. Should he tell her about June? Yes, of course he should. He should call her right this minute, he should—

"Daddy!"

Giles whirled around to see his perky, blond daughter. Even at two o'clock in the morning, Bunny looked perky.

"What are you doing here?" was what they both said.

"You go first, Bunns," Giles said. "Did you come to see Mommy?"

"I suppose I didn't. Well, maybe I did, but I didn't know I did." Bunny darted a sideways glace at her mother. Tears welled in her eyes. "Is Mommy sick?"

The simple-minded question puzzled Giles, though he didn't realize he had asked a rather obvious one himself. "I don't know, Bunny. Well, I mean, I know why I came here. Or did you already know?"

Bunny leaned her head to one side and frowned. "What did you say?"

"It's nothing. Tell me, did you ever hear from Daniel? I've been running about all night searching for him. Where on earth could he have gone?"

Again, tears flowed from Bunny's mascara-smudged eyes. "That's why I came looking for you. I stopped by the big house first, and that's when I saw Felicity's note. Oh Daddy! I have something so bad to tell you and Mommy."

"Dear God, is Daniel dead?"

Bunny shook her head. Her golden ponytail wagged from side to side. "Right now, I wish he were," she said, just before her tears exploded into a full-blown crying jag.

"Bunnykins, what on earth?"

"Danny's cheating on me, Daddy!"

"What did you just say?" A furtive backwards glance at his comatose wife preceded his next remark. "How can you be so sure?"

Bunny blew her cute nose on a piece of powder pink tissue. Then, with a whimper, she blinked back her tears to compose herself. "I'm not stupid. Sometimes I think Danny doesn't think I'm paying attention, and sometimes, well, sometimes I'm not, but sometimes I am. And Daddy, women have a sixth sense about cheating men. I know I do. I must have gotten it from Mommy, don't you think?"

At this sudden confession, Giles felt a sudden jolt—a vile mix of fear, and guilt, but worst of all, deception—from his own daughter. Why or even how he managed to face June's ghostly countenance at this moment, he couldn't have said. But at this moment, he did so. What exactly was Bunny trying to tell him? Exactly how much did Junebug know? But, he decided, enough of that kind of speculation. Now, he must get back to Daniel.

"Bunns," Giles said in a muffled whisper, "if you really think Daniel is cheating, do you know who she is?" For some incomprehensible reason, he found himself holding his breath. Why, he couldn't have said.

"Oh yes, Daddy." Bunny's blond head bobbed up and down with conviction. "It's that redheaded reporter, Gabby Knowes."

Giles vaguely remembered her. Such a nuisance she was. Still, he breathed a sigh of relief. No one suspected Leila, or so it seemed. No one except Rocco, but he trusted Rocco with his life. Besides Rocco, no one was the wiser, no matter what Dr. Hart said. His secret remained safe.

In his heart of hearts, that secret dictated his every thought, his every action. He lived in fear of the day when some busybody—like Gabby Knowes—discovered their affair-because then, it would have to end. The Junebug simply couldn't endure it. *Wait a minute...*

No, he had this all wrong. In fact, his worst fear was that Leila would leave him for a younger, better looking man. That would be so humiliating. He simply couldn't endure it. Of course, he wouldn't tolerate such shabby treatment. It would have to end.

He stared at his snoring wife. How many times had June cheated Death? Frankly, he'd lost count. If he lost Leila, he would surely die before the Junebug. Right after he killed the younger, better looking man, that is.

Nine

"You'd better go now, Felicity," Rocco said. His alert, dark eyes seemed riveted on the closed white enameled door.

Felicity arched a penciled eyebrow in askance. "The Mr. Dingwerth, I don't think he knows you're here."

"So?"

"So, maybe you should go before he sees you."

"Why?" Rocco sighed in exasperation. "Dios mío," he said under his breath. Would this night never end? Again, he thought, how much did Felicity know?

The door opened, and Giles tiptoed into the hall. Rocco couldn't comprehend the reason for his tentative demeanor. But, that wasn't all that puzzled him. Although Mr. Dingwerth seemed genuinely glad to see Felicity, there was something intangible that eluded him. Rocco would have bet his rosary that Felicity and Mr. Dingwerth shared some private secret; a certain something even he, Rocco, did not know of—yet. He could feel it in the air. What did they know?

"Ah, Felicity, thank the heavens," Giles said. He opened his arms to embrace her in a ritual hug. "I don't know what we would have done without you to assist my poor, helpless wife. I want you to know how much I appreciate it."

"You do?" Felicity said. Her voice snapped with hostility. Rocco thought Mr. Dingwerth noticed it, but just as easily, chose to ignore it. "You know," Felicity continued, "I wish you had come home sooner, sir. We barely made it in time. One of these days…"

"So they say, dear," Giles said. "You'll feel better after a good night's sleep. I know I will. Rocco, could you bring the car around?"

Rocco welcomed the opportunity to excuse himself from the confrontation, but he couldn't erase the negative vibes between Felicity and Mr. Dingwerth from his mind. In his bewildered, bedraggled state, he reasoned, he could be imagining anything. Probably was. Still, when he guided the Mercedes up to the curb of the hospital, he noticed the pair stood a chilly distance apart, certainly not conducive to a friendly conversation. Something told him it was time to open his eyes and ears.

The ride home proved tense, despite the unanimous fatigue. Few words were exchanged; Mr. Dingwerth occupied the passenger seat, Felicity the back. On the horizon, dawn threatened to break. When they approached the massive front gates emblazoned with the golden-gilt "D's", Felicity popped the question. "Mr. Dingwerth, where were you when I called tonight?"

Mr. Dingwerth started at the sudden question—his shoulders and neck jerked backwards, and his eyes had the telltale panicked stare—and Rocco wondered if Felicity had noticed the same thing. No matter. His response revealed all. "Why, I was out searching for Daniel, as Mrs. Dingwerth requested."

"But, we needed you. Why didn't you come home?"

"Felicity, I've had about enough annoyance tonight, don't you think? I didn't come home because I was searching for someone."

"Did you find them?"

"Why yes, yes I did."

Felicity folded her calloused hands in her lap for a second, just before she glanced at the massive house. A light frost coated the expansive lawn. "I thought so," was all she said.

Without a word, Rocco hustled to open the front passenger door.

Leila couldn't sleep. Her dark, almond-shaped eyes cracked to view the time on the bedside alarm clock. Four thirty. What was bothering her? She punched the limp pillow into a ball and plopped her head into the feathery lump. Lots of things, she decided. First, there was Carlos. Before this trip to Missouri, he never bothered her so much. She should divorce him, but divorce in Venezuela, well, it was messy, it was against her religion, and she considered it, well, incompatible with her social standing. Besides, there was no need. That is, until now. What had changed?

She lay on her back and studied the ceiling fan. She was tempted to light a cigarette, but didn't. What was wrong with her? Until yesterday, she'd had a cool control over the men in her life, kind of like pieces in a game of chess. What she was feeling now was a confusing mix of detachment, tolerance and passion—yes, passion.

The detachment made her feel grounded. This was her, Leila Bolivar, distant, controlled and controlling. The tolerance, well, she recognized that, and, she didn't like it. She didn't like to admit she would tolerate a man like Giles Dingwerth for…what? For money, prestige, pretty perks of the position, she supposed. In some people's eyes, she supposed, that made her a prostitute—but, not in her own. In her viewpoint, she was simply doing what many women all over the world did every day, including the Junebug. Were those women prostitutes?

She sat up in bed and reached for her cigarettes. She simply had to have one. She blew a puff of smoke into the stuffy air. What bothered her so much?

She didn't recognize it, and yet, she craved it. The passion blindsided her. The smoldering desire, the obsession she felt for a man she barely knew, this was not like her. The sleek young man with his dazzling smile had resurrected a side of her that she didn't know she had. Thinking of him like this, she ached to see him. When? She hadn't arranged that critical detail before he left. She would do that now.

No matter that it was only 6:04 a.m. Leila would call his cell phone and leave a message, that's what she would do. Not on the hotel phone, of course. Nothing could ever be traced to Room

1204 that way. Leila stood poised at the narrow window, her cell phone pressed to her ear. She watched a fly scamper across the dusty sill. The gray dawn peeked through the clouds.

Four rings, and she would leave her message. For a moment, she thought she heard footsteps outside her door. But her attention was soon riveted on her pending phone call. What? Who had just answered the phone?

"Hello," said a woman's voice. "Who is this?" the voice screeched.

Leila had not expected this response. Had she dialed the wrong number? No, she didn't think so. "Daniel Hunter?" she said. "Is he there?"

"Yes, he is. This is his wife. Who is this?"

His wife? Daniel Hunter's wife? It must be The Bunny. The fly buzzed in circles around the whirring ceiling fan.

"Who is this?" the voice repeated, louder this time.

"Wrong number," Leila said. "Very sorry."

The blades of the fan smashed the fly.

Leila hung up in haste, and took a deep breath. There was no time to contemplate her newfound knowledge. The bedside telephone was ringing—what an annoying brrring it made. She picked up the receiver just to end it. Yet, the annoyance had only just begun.

"Hello?" she said.

"Leila, darling," Giles said, "when can I see you?"

Bunny lounged in her pink chenille bathrobe, trying to read the front page of the newspaper while she ate. In a way, she hated to distance herself from the marshmallow shapes that floated in her cereal bowl, but…it was really the only way she could stand to read the news. Daddy always advised her to keep up with current affairs. She sighed and tucked one foot under her tanned body. She tried so hard to expand her mind—really.

Yet, in some things, she felt she was light years ahead of her more intellectual friends. Take last night, for example. She knew

Danny was lying to her then, just as he fibbed to her this morning before he left the house. Of course he was cheating on her. Did he think she was stupid? One thing bothered her. As much as Bunny hated to admit it, the woman's voice on the phone this morning didn't sound like the redhead. She gasped, and set her spoon down besides her half-empty cereal bowl. Could Danny have two girlfriends? Was it possible?

How she wished she could call Mommy. Mommy wouldn't want to hear anything bad about Danny, though. She always took his side, and Bunny never understood her reasons. That settled it. She would just have to call Daddy. Glancing down at the wilting cereal floating in the blue-grey tinged milk, she sighed and padded over to the white wall phone in her fuzzy pink slippers. She was about to hang up when finally, her father's secretary picked up the phone.

"Dingwerth Distinctive Designs," the woman groaned.

"I already know that, silly," Bunny giggled. "Is Daddy there?"

"Who is this?"

Bunny thrust her firm hip to one side and jabbed one manicured hand into her narrow waist. Who did she think it was? "It's Bunny! Is Daddy there?"

It was the secretary's turn to giggle. "Uh, okay. Bunny for Daddy."

Bunny studied the remains of the soggy Lucky Charms in her cereal bowl, now floating in completely discolored milk. Ever since the marshmallow shapes and colors had changed, Lucky Charms tasted, well, different. If Bunny Dingwerth knew anything well, she knew the shapes and colors of her marshmallow Lucky Charms. When she was a little girl, for example, there had been yellow moons, pink hearts and green four leaf clovers. The milk used to turn pink. That, in Bunny's opinion, was normal. Finally, she heard a click on the line.

"Giles Dingwerth."

Again, Bunny giggled. "I already knew that."

"Bunny? Sweetheart, is something wrong?"

"No, Daddy. Well, really, I don't know. I wanted to ask you something."

"Can it wait, honey? I'm trying to meet a deadline right now. Later tonight we could—"

"No, Daddy. I need to know right now."

"What is that, Bunnykins? Ask me anything. Anything at all. Just ask away. Quickly, please."

"How can I tell, I mean for sure, if Danny's cheating on me? What is that noise? Are you alright?"

"Bunny, uh, why don't you ask your mother? She—"

"Daddy, you know why. Mommy's in a coma."

"Oh, right. Right." There was a pause, then… "I should have remembered that. The truth is, sweetheart, you can't. Some men are very good at hiding this sort of thing, you know."

"Well, I know he's interested in that nuisance reporter with the red hair. Kind of looks like a scarecrow, doesn't she?"

"What? Well, we'll put a stop to this, honey. You just leave it all to me. Now, if that's all—"

"Wait, Daddy. It's not."

"You just told me all I need to know."

"No. I didn't. A woman called Danny on his cell phone this morning, early. Like, six thirty or something like that."

"Six thirty?"

"Yes! And after the night he had, too. But, she didn't sound like the redhead. She sounded Spanish or Mexican, I don't know which. They're the same, aren't they?"

"They're not at all the same, Bunns." Again, a pause lapsed. "Wait a minute. What did you say?"

"I said, she sounded, hmmm, okay I'll say…Spanish, how's that? Daddy, are you there?"

"Yes, yes, I'm here. Well, what did she say?"

"I don't know. I would ask Mommy what to do, but well, she's in a coma."

"No, Bunny, no. It's better you asked me. Especially under the circumstances."

"You mean Mommy's coma?"

"No, I mean…yes, that's exactly what I mean. Bunny, tell me the truth. Have you told anyone else about this phone call-anyone but me?"

"No, Daddy. No one."

"Good. You just leave it to me. No one else needs to know a thing."

"O-okay. You won't hurt Danny, will you?"

"I don't know," Giles said.

Brock shook his tousled hair and studied his graying blond locks in the half-length mirror. Lowlights, highlights—so many choices out there, really. He needed dimension, that's what he needed. After all, he thought, while his tapered fingers combed through his layered cut, these days, he was all about change. Why, he'd dropped nearly eight pounds, he was drinking regular coffee again, listening to the Eagles—can you believe it?—and then, there was his boldest, most adventurous move, his new life with divorcee Angela Hart. He'd even frightened himself with that decision. Even now, he wasn't sure that he'd done the right thing. He missed Marc dreadfully. There, he admitted it, okay?

He missed the way they used to order Chinese and watch re-runs of old *I Love Lucy* and *Gilligan's Island* shows. Angela didn't want to do that. Angela wanted Brock to style her hair at least once a day, sometimes twice, and reassure her of her amazing, eternal beauty. This, Brock could do. What Brock couldn't do, he decided, was mean what he said. STRESSED to the MAX—incidentally, the name of his newest hair spray—well, he couldn't have described the any situation better. One peek at the word "stress" in his mental dictionary revealed Angela's name in bold letters.

"How's my favorite gossip junkie?"

A gust of icy air blustered into the salon. Oh jeepers, thought Brock. After the weekend he'd had, he'd completely forgotten. Well, his own personal highlights would have to wait. Penny Brown, first appointment of the day, had just arrived. He spritzed his hair with a burst of hairspray, just before she flopped into his vinyl chair. Though they were alone in the shop, he leaned down and whispered, "It's been wild, Brown, trust me. And oh, uh, I'm not with Marc anymore." In the mirror straight ahead, Brock watched Penny's hazel eyes widen.

"But, why? You were the perfect couple!"

Again, Brock combed through his locks, this time with trembling fingers. His voice remained a hushed whisper. "I've changed completely, Brown. I'm with Angela Hart now."

Penny scowled, and glanced around the empty salon. "Brock, why are we whispering? Anyway, I don't believe you. It's your business, but Angela Hart is a scheming shrew, a phony, plastic wannabe, a… Oh, I get it, did she promise you something? It's money, isn't it?"

Brock sniffed. "I can't be bought."

"Everyone has a price."

"Not me. I'm simply reinventing myself, Brown."

"What was so wrong with you before? I liked you, Marc certainly liked you, and gobs of your clients liked you enough to help you build a successful business. I mean, take a look at this place. Why mess with success?"

Brock's shoulders slumped in weary resignation. He wasn't sure he could explain his metamorphosis, because in truth, he didn't understand it himself. "It's like this. I'm tired."

"You're tired? Tired of what?"

Brock's thin lips curved into a wan half-smile. "I'm tired of the whole struggle. Everyday. People treating me like I'm a freak the second they suspect I'm gay. I'm tired, Brown! I'm tired of trying to convince other people that I want the same things for my life that they want. You bet I'm tired. But, that's all going to change now. I'll just be straight, and I won't have to put up with their attitude."

"Oh, I get it. You think that you won't get tired trying to be something you're not."

"That was mean."

"Okay, Brock, it's your business. Just work your magic on this mane of mine. But, I'll say it again. I liked you the way you were. And just one more thing. I think you'll find that life with Angela Hart is going to be nothing but a struggle that makes you nothing but tired."

"It's worth a try, because I'm already worn out. You know what else? Maybe there's another side to me, you know?"

Penny settled into the vinyl chair and closed her eyes. "You don't need one, Brock."

"We'll see, Brown. We'll see."

Ten

"This cereal tastes funny." Bunny scrunched up her perky nose and stared across the breakfast table, where Dan slouched in hung over silence. A mug of lukewarm hot chocolate sat before him, untouched. Even in his weakened condition, however, he knew he was required to say something. It didn't really matter what; he knew that, too.

"Bunny, of course it tastes funny. Lucky Charms do that." Dan covered his pallid face with his hand. It was almost painful to watch a grown woman poke at a cereal bowl brimming with blue marshmallow moons and pink hearts, not to mention soggy green leprechaun hats. Had they discussed this ritual before the memorable mega wedding? Dan couldn't remember now. He didn't think so. How could he have known it would be The Thing that drove him to distraction every single morning?

Now, she dangled a spoonful of limp oat cereal and blue tinged milk beneath his congested nose. Thank God for small favors. "Here," she said, "you taste this."

"No, Bunny. I can't even look at food this morning."

"Well, it's your own fault." Bunny shoved the mess into her own mouth and swallowed, wincing. A dribble of violet-blue milk dribbled down her chin. "Daddy searched and searched for you last night, you know. Which reminds me, where were you yesterday afternoon?"

Dan coughed. His voice was hoarse when he finally spoke. "I was at work. Where else would I be?"

Bunny flung her empty spoon across the table. "Liar! Daddy told me you weren't at work. Besides, I already knew it. Penny and Candy saw you at the club yesterday afternoon, talking on your cell phone." Her green eyes narrowed with suspicion. "You were with that redheaded reporter, weren't you?"

Dan raised his head. "What? That's ridiculous. I don't even know who you're talking about."

"You're such a liar. Don't you think I know something's going on?"

"You're crazy!"

"Am I? Let this crazy woman remind you of one thing, Danny Hunter. All of this," she said, gesturing to the sumptuous surroundings, "belongs to us because of me. Me and my Daddy. We let you have some because you make us happy. Remember that, 'kay?"

Dan got up and sighed. He had a tornado spinning in his head right now. Of one thing he was absolutely certain. He had to get out of this marriage, one way or another. But how? Divorce? He guessed it was looming on his horizon. He would lose everything. The Dingwerths would ruin him and everything he'd ever worked for unless, unless...

His weary gaze lingered on the half eaten bowl of Lucky Charms. Slowly, the seed burrowed itself deep in his drowsy brain. Maybe, just maybe, he was onto something.

Funny tasting, huh?

Leila wasn't sure about anything anymore. Here she was, rushing to get to her 9 a.m. photo shoot, and she couldn't think straight. There had been a time when she'd thought her arrangement with Giles was perfect, at least for her present needs. Maybe even future wants, who knew? In a flash, she reminded herself. She'd felt exactly the same way about Carlos in the beginning, hadn't she? Where had those ardent feelings gone? The buried memories refreshed, it was hard to apply her eyeshadow. Damn

Carlos. With all these distractions, she couldn't even stand to look herself in the mirror.

One thing was certain. She had to have Dan Hunter in her life. The question was, what to do about Giles Dingwerth? Until Dan, she hadn't really thought about doing anything about him, but now…well, he was becoming more demanding, more controlling, and way too restrictive of her personal time. And that meant less time with Dan.

Like that phone call just now. She supposed that was when she realized she resented Giles' impositions. Still, there were the extras he provided. She admired the new sapphire ring on her right ring finger, her latest Giles Gift. It glistened, like Leila herself, even in the dim lights of the hotel room. She glanced at the sidewalk beneath her room.

Just as she had suspected, Rocco parked at the curb in the Mercedes, waiting for her. She would think more about her dilemma on the way to work. One thing was certain. With the three lovers—Carlos, Giles and Dan—in her life, one would simply have to go. Still, she would have to carefully consider the implications of her next move. With Carlos, she enjoyed security and respectability, Giles provided luxurious wealth, and with Dan, she had unearthed a passion she hadn't imagined she could feel for any man—until Daniel Hunter.

She grabbed her tote bag and purse and dashed into the hall, heading for the elevator. Her head spun; her thoughts raced. She wished she hadn't agreed to see Giles tonight, but he'd insisted. Well, tonight she would. The elevator doors opened. Even in the clear sunlight, her dilemma remained cloudy.

Giles sat at the breakfast table alone this morning; well, not quite. Felicity, bless her soul, was more vigilant today. He appreciated that about her, almost as much as he savored the relative peace, however temporary. He'd been fooled before, he reminded himself, while sipping strong, black coffee from a bone china cup. June had had numerous near death experiences, but always, she'd survived them.

Well, he didn't really want the Junebug to die, not permanently. Just for the remainder of his physical life would do quite nicely. He spread orange marmalade on his dry white toast and gazed out the leaded glass at the expansive lawn. The thing was, thoughts like these made him feel that he was a wicked, evil man. Why…why, *that* he was not!

He straightened his back against the wooden slat in the mahogany dining chair. He was Giles Dingwerth, President of Dingwerth Distinctive Designs, son of Giles Merriweather Dingwerth, former President of Dingwerth Distinctive Designs, grandson of Giles Everding Dingwerth, former former President of Dingwerth Distinctive Designs, great-grandson of Giles Harrison Dingwerth, founder of Dingwerth Distinctive Designs…well now, a person with such a grand legacy simply couldn't be evil now, could he? No. Of course not. Giles blotted his sticky mouth with his starched napkin. He took a deep breath and relaxed. He felt so much better.

"Mr. Dingwerth?"

For a reason Giles couldn't explain, Felicity's soft voice startled him. "Yes, what is it?"

"Will you be going to the hospital today to visit Mrs. Dingwerth?"

For propriety's sake, Giles knew he should feign indignation. "Of course. Didn't you think I would plan to visit my ailing wife? Don't I always?"

Felicity's lined face bore no expression; neither did her voice. "It's just that Rocco called, sir. He would like to know of your plans."

"Well, I'll call him, then. Why all the fuss?" At that moment, Giles didn't quite know how to interpret the sudden suspicion in Felicity's eyes. In the next one, however, it became clear.

"Rocco says he must pick up a lady at two o'clock for you. He wants you to let him know of your plans for today." Felicity stared at the floor. "Since Mrs. Dingwerth became ill so, you know, so quickly."

"Look at me, Felicity. I'm sure you know that my relationship with my 'lady' as you call her, is not a simple friendship. As I told you when it started six months ago or so, a man of my position often has such a lady in his life. It's not such a big deal. You do know Mrs. Dingwerth is quite prone to illness, real or imagined, and that she makes things worse when she breaks her diet, which is just as often. Besides, it wouldn't surprise either of us, or Rocco either for that matter, if Mrs. Dingwerth knew of my 'lady.' Has she ever mentioned anything to you?"

Felicity was tempted, Giles could tell, but no, she wouldn't tip her hand. She wasn't talking, not yet. Instead, she simply shook her head. "No."

"Very well, then. Please dust up the guest room in the west wing."

"Yes, sir."

"And Felicity?"

"Sir?"

"Fresh sheets on the bed?"

"*Sí.*"

"Good. I'll call Rocco, don't fret about that. By the way, has Bunny called? I was wondering about Daniel."

"No, sir. No word from Miss Bunny."

"Funny, don't you think so? I mean, after all that's happened?" Giles waited, and waited some more. Felicity didn't utter a single word. She simply turned and began to clear the breakfast dishes from the table, and somehow, Giles sensed the reason for her silence.

After all, there was still a lot going on, wasn't there?

"Any word from your ex?"

Gabby leaned closer to Marc across the polished marble counter. It was just before 9 a.m., and the lobby of the Hotel Charlotte was still calm. Usually, things didn't pick up until just before noon. Today was no exception.

At the veiled reference to Brock, Marc's jaw stiffened. "Actually, yes, I have."

Oooh, thought Gabby, this would be good. After all, she loved nothing better than a good clean, dirty fight. She summoned her best soothing tone of voice. "Has something upset you?"

"Well," Marc said, "I wouldn't exactly say that, but…"

"What? What is it, Marc?"

Marc stared past her shoulder at something, well, eye-popping it seemed. "Isn't that Leila Bolivar?"

"Who?"

"You know, the model from South America. Leila Bolivar. Everyone says she's having an affair with Giles Dingwerth. But of course, you already knew that."

Gabby felt ecstatic! Her nerves had nerves. She lived for moments like this one, by golly. It was Christmas, and Marc here was Mr. Santa himself, because, true or not, if everyone already thought so, solid news like this belonged in the Gateway Gabette. "Tell me," she said, her gaze fixed on the lithe, glamorous Leila, her hair whipping in the breeze, her long, graceful legs striding toward the waiting Mercedes. Together, she and Marc watched as the Mercedes sped away, and for a few seconds, they were inexplicably speechless.

"Gabby, I really do have work to do," Marc said, rearranging the mounds of receipts that littered the cluttered desk before him.

"But, we need to talk."

"About? I've told you all I know. Now, shoo."

"Listen to you! Hardly one word about Brock, and you expect me to leave. Come on, Marc. Everyone wants to know about Angela Hart, you know that."

"What's to know? You know, this is really painful for me, Gabby, do you realize that?"

"I can appreciate that. And…so can my readers. Don't you think they want to know about the cunning temptress that ruined your perfect life?"

"Well, if you put it that way."

"I thought so. Let's have it. It's coffee break time."

"Hmmm. What's in it for me?"

"What do you want? Maybe I can get it for you."

Again, Marc's gaze was focused on something behind her, what, Gabby couldn't say. That is, until she turned to see a rumpled Dan Hunter approach the desk. Great. The donut guy. Marc leaned across the counter to whisper. "You asked me what I want? Now that is someone I would like to meet. I just love his smile." Marc smoothed his hair and smiled at Dan. "Can I help you?"

Dan looked breathless enough for the both of them. He edged in beside Gabby and pressed his chapped hands against the cold marble counter. "Leila Bolivar, please? Do you have her room number handy? I seem to have misplaced it."

"I'm sorry?" Marc said.

Dan coughed and cleared his throat. "Leila Bolivar, the model. Has she checked out?"

Marc raised an eyebrow and sneaked a quick look in Gabby's direction. "Why no, I don't have any record of that," Marc said, "though I believe she stepped out for a bit. Would you like me to ring her room?"

"You say she stepped out?"

"I believe so, sir. I'm sure she'll be back sometime today. Is there any message?"

Gabby thought Dan appeared to be in another place, far, far away. Suddenly, he reached for his cell phone and stepped towards the revolving door, shaking his head from side to side, as if to say "no." All he did say was simply, "thanks." In a flash, he was on the phone. "Leila? Hey, it's me, Dan. Did you call early this morning?" He laughed. "I thought it was you. How about tonight? Why not? See what you can do, okay? I mean, I'm free tonight. My wife's going out for awhile. Yeah sure, call me back."

Gabby and Marc watched as Dan strolled into the hotel coffee shop. "I thought you said she was having an affair with Giles Dingwerth," Gabby said. "You got your facts mixed up."

"Don't think so. Why don't you find out? This is right up your alley. Besides, you don't like Dan Hunter anyway."

Marc drummed his fingers on the counter. "Wait a minute. I might be able to help you after all."

"What are you going to do?"

"I'm going to call Brock."

"Because?"

"Because. Maybe I've been hanging around you too long, who knows? Or maybe because he once mentioned that Dr. Hart took care of Mrs. Dingwerth."

"You devil, you."

Dr. Hart scanned his clipboard for some last minute comments. He was well aware that his patient's husband, Giles Dingwerth, IV, lest he need to be reminded, fidgeted before his eyes, literally aching to leave. Lunch date, perhaps? He knew he was being perverse, but, he decided to prolong the consultation; watch Giles dangle like a spider from a sticky, tangled web.

Come to think of it, hadn't Angela mentioned something about Giles Dingwerth a while back? Angela prattled on so much. What was it that she'd said? He would think of it eventually. "Well," he said, "do you have any further questions? If you like, I could probably send June home around five or so today…"

"Oh no! No. NO."

"Well Giles, really." Dr. Hart chuckled, an uncomfortable moment for the both of them. "You do want her to come home, don't you?"

"What I mean is, doctor, I want her to be ready to come home. She's not an easy woman to live with anyway, as I'm sure you can appreciate."

"What do you mean by that?"

"Only that you had a bit of trouble yourself along those lines, didn't you? And, you know June. Women are difficult, by God. They're moody, they're irrational, they're demanding…so unlike a man. Well, you know…now, there's my phone. Would you excuse me for a minute?"

Dr. Hart tapped his pen against the metal clip on the board. What if he had refused? Eavesdropping as he did now, however, he was so glad he hadn't. Giles sounded a wee bit upset, well a lot really, and he was making no effort to conceal his angst. "Well, when can I see you then?" he said. "What? Stomach flu? Well, I'll come over and keep you company. Oh, my wife's fine, really. I just saw her. She was, uh, sleeping. That's what I said. I saw her sleeping. Look, Leila, I can't talk now. I'll call you later. Fine, then. I'll call you tomorrow." Giles flipped his cell phone shut and turned around to face Dr. Hart. His face was flushed a bright pink.

Leila? Dr. Hart felt confused. Had he heard Giles say Leila? That was it! June Dingwerth mentioned her name at least a dozen times since her admission, before she'd gone into a coma. Now he recalled how she'd wept while she recounted Giles' hushed conversations with Felicity, that ended when she entered the room, the lies Giles told her that never added up to anything, the anonymous phone calls, when all June could do was say hello, hello, hello, over and over again.

Now June, he'd assured her, you're not well, we both know Giles loves you desperately, he'd never do anything to hut you, etc., etc. He'd said the same thing to various other patients in the same situation.

Whatever June Dingwerth was, she was not stupid or overly romantic. She didn't buy it. "Dr. Hart," she'd said in her raspy smoker's voice, "it's that model Leila Bolivar that Giles wants, not me."

Even then, he'd wondered why June elected now to confide this scandal to him, as obviously sick as she was. Couldn't they discuss this at a later date, he'd asked? And then, he recalled now, she had said the strangest thing.

"I just want you to know Giles might not mind it very much if I were to suddenly, shall we say, fade into the sunset." June had sat straight up in the bed, her eyes wide with clarity. "If I should suddenly die, doctor, it might not be an accident. My death might not happen in the way it was meant to. That's what I'm saying."

"June, are you saying Giles would like to kill you?" He recalled now how he had chuckled at the idea. "Do you hear yourself? With all respect, you're talking out of your head."

With her jaundiced complexion and tousled, tangled hair, he suspected she was losing her sanity. Now, with the flushed, sheepish husband standing before him, his mouth grew dry. He felt his teeth clench. He wasn't sure he knew the truth anymore. Besides, there was something worse.

He was beginning to believe that perhaps he didn't want to know the answer.

Eleven

"Angela?"

Angela Hart leaned against the kitchen counter, and sucked a lazy drag from her cigarette. Eugene bored her. Bored, bored, bored her! And now, he was on the phone again, just when she was preparing to serve Brock's favorite asparagus-mushroom quiche. She flipped the wide sleeve of her tangerine chiffon caftan away from her bony wrist, and sighed audibly into the receiver. "I have company, Eugene. This is not a good time."

She turned to see Brock entering the kitchen, clad in his black silk kimono. What a body—so taut and tanned—so unlike Eugene's pale, fleshy one. What did her soon to be ex-husband want? "What kind of emergency? Everything is an emergency to you, Eugene. That's why I left you, remember?"

She stubbed out her cigarette and popped a peppermint breath mint into her mouth. The quiche was getting cold. Eugene was babbling something about June Dingwerth, the old tart. Of course she remembered June. Who could forget that neurotic mess?

"Are you coming, baby?" Brock said, unfolding his napkin.

Angela loved it when he called her *baby*. She would have hung up on Eugene if their divorce was final, but alas… "Alright, alright, what is it? Who was Giles fooling around with? Well, it's just a rumor, Eugene. That's all. Brock heard it from a customer. That's right, he's a stylist. I said, a stylist, with style. Something you wouldn't know anything about."

What a pest. How could she, why would she, remember

anything about the Dingwerths? She just didn't care that much.

"Well, he's sitting right here, let me ask him." Angela covered the receiver with her long fingers. "Darling, do you remember who Giles Dingwerth was supposedly fooling around with? I mean, the gossip, you know."

Brock sipped white wine from a small goblet. "It's only a nasty rumor, darling."

"Brock, it's Eugene. I just want to get off the phone. Now."

"Fine. But, you didn't hear it from me. And, I'm not going to reveal my sources, either."

"Tick, tock, Brock—"

"Leila Bolivar."

"The model? What would she want with Giles Dingwerth?"

Brock took another sip from his glass. "My lips are sealed." He gestured toward the succulent quiche, browned to perfection. "May I?"

"Go ahead, I'll be right there." Angela uncovered the receiver. "Eugene, are you sitting down? Alright, it's just a rumor. Leila Bolivar. The model, right. How should I know? Look, I've got to go. And Eugene, my lawyer will be calling yours, probably, oh, tomorrow morning. Yeah, you too."

Angela replaced the receiver and took a place at the table. Brock still looked good, but somehow, the quiche didn't. Not anymore. Calls from Eugene did that to her.

"Are you alright?" Brock nudged the quiche toward her plate. "You must be hungry after our little rendezvous." He winked at her and cut a chunk of quiche with his fork. She watched him chew it, brushing crumbs from the table into his napkin. He was right. The afternoon had been good. The quiche looked, well, good. So, what was wrong?

She couldn't put her finger on it. She loathed herself for the thought, but after speaking to her ex-husband, she couldn't deny the difference between the two men. What was it? In some ways, Brock was a better lover than Eugene, wasn't he? Yes, but...well... there was that sneaky suspicion Brock was only trying to please her, that he wasn't satisfied, really satisfied with her at all. Not like Eugene had been. Was she imagining things? She didn't think so.

Would this be a good time to discuss it with Brock? She gazed at her handsome, younger lover and, for once, quickly decided.

No. She didn't think so.

Like sludge through a drain, the words ran through his memory. Dr. Hart felt confused. *"Leila, I can't talk now. I'll call you later,"* and *"Leila Bolivar. The model, right. How should I know?"* Like a tornado, sordid thoughts whisked through his mind, causing him to jump to hasty, and he reminded himself, probably wrong conclusions regarding the Dingwerths. Was June's life in danger? What should he do about it?

He drove slowly, headed for his lonely apartment, leased in desperation and haste the day after Angela and he separated. Heavy clouds crowded the dusky sky. The wind gusted through the brittle leaves, whistling through some random crevices in his temporary car, rented while his Cadillac was being repaired after a hit and run accident in the hospital parking lot.

Finally, he reached his destination, and shook his head in disgust. Even as he made his way to the long, low building he called home, at least for now Giles' remark stung his ears. *"...you had a bit of trouble yourself along those lines, didn't you, doctor?"*

Dr. Hart jabbed his tinny key into the cheap lock, his rounded shoulders slumping with fatigue. Giles Dingwerth was right. Who was he to judge anyone? Yes, he thought, while he poured himself a glass of Cabernet, he'd had trouble with Angela, but that didn't mean...it didn't mean he couldn't judge reality for what it clearly was. He knew what June had said. He'd heard Giles on the phone. He'd even talked to Angela—what a sacrifice that had been! He took a gulp of wine to fortify his nerves. There, that was better. What if June died? He took a deep breath and sighed.

Maybe she wouldn't.

He peered through the dirty blinds at the serene cemetery across the street from his apartment. The granite headstones fairly gleamed in the brilliant moonlight. June Dingwerth's bony finger had rung Death's doorbell twice—that he knew of—but always, she had recovered. There was no reason to believe this time would be any different. That is, unless someone didn't want her to. He drained his wine glass, and headed for the back bedroom to undress. He had a sickening feeling he knew who that person might be.

The phone rang before he unbuttoned his starched shirt. Eleven o'clock was late by most people's standards, but not Dr. Hart's. Any time of the day or night, his phone rang. Why not now? "Yes," he said in a low voice, his fingers curling around the receiver. He had a feeling he knew who it was. He wasn't disappointed. "Hello Marc," he said with a twinkle in his brown eyes.

Luther wasn't absolutely sure now, but he was sure enough. He'd never seen that pink Cadillac before, but he was sure he'd seen that white guy somewhere, at least once. Was it yesterday, or the day before? Here he was, back again, for the happy hour. The thing was, Luther wondered, what should he charge for his fine parking?

He took a swig of root beer from an amber bottle and wiped his mouth with the back of his hand. He guessed the thing to do would be to ask the guy if he intended to leave it overnight. Yep, that would help him decide how much to charge.

Hey, the guy was walking toward him now. "How much do I owe you?" he heard him say.

As he got closer, Luther noticed the gash in his face, and the bruises on his face. A mild breeze ruffled his brown hair. Even with his face all banged up like that, Luther still thought he was a nice looking guy—for a white guy, that is. Luther sniffed the air. Wowser, somebody sure had a lot of cologne on, and all Luther could think was, it wasn't him.

Luther had to fight with himself to avoid staring at that gash. He couldn't help himself. He just had to ask. "Hey, what'd you do to your face?" he said. He could tell he'd struck a very raw nerve.

"Give me a break. I was in an accident, okay? That okay with you? Now, how much do I owe you?"

Until just now, Luther had actually felt sorry for this guy. But right now, well... "That depends."

"On what?"

"What you think? On how long you park. Lots of people use my fine parking, bye the bye."

The white guy with the gash in his forehead was thumbing through his wallet now. A frown crinkled his brow. "Thought I had more cash on me than that." He handed Luther two twenty-dollar bills. "Look, I'm sorry I was a jerk a minute ago. I'm driving this heinous car that belongs to my mother-in-law, and let me tell you, I feel like a fool."

Luther took another swig of root beer, and again, wiped his mouth with the back of his hand. "A fool? Why? It runs, don't it?"

"Well, yeah."

"What's the matter, then?"

"The color, man. It's pink. It's not me, okay? Look, I've got to go. Put it in the overnight, willya?" He winked at Luther with a twinkle in his eye, and Luther understood. What Luther didn't understand was him using his mother-in-law's car to do it. The guy was either crazy or stupid, whoever he was. Whoever he was, he was planning on one long happy hour.

He had barely climbed behind the steering wheel when he saw them; it was the black Mercedes, with Rocky driving. Man, this was weird, is what it was. Now, it was all coming back to him. These guys had shown up on the same day before, maybe was it last week or so? That white guy's name was Dan. Hey, maybe somebody was being followed, how about that? He waited while Rocky hustled up to the driver's window on the Cadillac.

"Wassup?" Luther said. "I'll be with ya'll soon as I park this Caddy in the overnight."

Right away, Luther knew he had said something wrong. He didn't know what, but Rocky looked like he had seen a ghost. Couldn't let him stop him from doing what he told Dan he would do, though. If Rocky done seen a ghost, Luther figured he could see one all by himself.

They were still there when he returned, Rocky and that white-haired guy he liked to drive around for fun. Luther walked around to Rocco's open window. Rocco waved a fifty-dollar bill in front of his face. "Want to tell us about the driver of the pink Cadillac?"

The fifty looked tempting—easy too. But, what in the… "Look, you want to tell me what's going on here?" he said.

"No," Giles said. "We would like for you to tell us."

Luther had been around enough to know at least one thing. Anybody willing to pay cash to tell him what was going on must think that something ba-a-ad was going down. Luther studied the fifty and decided Mr. Overnight might be worth a hundred, what do you think gentlemen? Of course, he didn't have a whole lot of information to divulge, or he would have gone higher. Sure looked to him like these guys had a few bucks. He waited while Giles peeled off another fifty. Rocco placed it in Luther's palm. "Okay for you?" Rocco said.

Luther grinned. "Sure. It's just fine. You boys up for a root beer?" As he spoke, he noticed Giles' face assume the shade of a beet. His expression was grim, though contained.

"First of all sir," he said, "you should know that the Cadillac belongs to my wife. At the moment, June is too ill to drive, and so I suppose young Daniel borrowed her car. Yes, I suppose that's the way it must have gone."

"Well, looks to me like you got it all worked out for yourself then," Luther said. "I'll just be on my way."

"Not quite so fast," Giles said. "I believe you were well paid for your time here. Did Daniel happen to tell you where he was going?"

"Overnight?" Rocco said.

Luther thought for a moment, and realized Dan had never

actually told him he was going to the Hotel Charlotte, or to a cocktail hour. Luther had only assumed as much. After all, it was where he went the last time, wasn't it? "Can't exactly say," said Luther, "because he didn't."

"But you did put June's Cadillac in the overnight parking?" Giles said.

"Yessir, I parked a Cadillac in the fine overnight parking, because that's what the man say he want." Luther shrugged. "But, he could always come back early now. People do that."

"Tell you what," Giles said. "I'd like to stop and check on something at the Hotel Charlotte. Rocco, could you please pull my car into a space?"

"Hey, just toss me the keys there, and I'll pull it in for ya'll," Luther said.

"No," Giles said, with a stern undertone in his voice. "Rocco will do it. In fact, he will wait for me while I pay a short visit. You don't mind, do you, Rocco?"

"No, sir." Rocco guided the Mercedes into the nearest spot.

Luther sensed their distrust. Well, he guessed he didn't blame them. He was keeping the hundred bucks, though. And, so it was that he said nothing when he happened to spy Dan with a beautiful dark-haired beauty, strolling down the opposite side of the street, even as Giles and Rocco strode into the Hotel Charlotte.

He grabbed his bottle of root beer and finished it off. When he looked up, neither Giles and Rocco, nor Dan and his lady friend was anywhere to be seen. Anyways, it was time for him to get back to work and stop his playing with these fools. He didn't like any of 'em too much anyways.

"Why don't we just take your car?" Leila said, her slender body pressed firmly beside Dan's. The fierce November wind whipped their flushed faces while they stood beside the curb, waiting to hail a taxi.

"It's a long story," Dan said, his arm raised to signal the oncoming cab. "Let's just say my car is in the shop."

"Okay," Leila said, "let's just say that. Right before we say why we couldn't just stay in my hotel room tonight."

A fine dust coated the backseat of the cab. Dan thought it smelled like an old man's closet. A used cigarette butt lay on the cold, hard floor. The brooding driver stared straight ahead, even as he gunned the engine and sped through a red traffic light. Dan wondered if he spoke English.

"Let's just say that tonight, it's my turn to entertain you," he said. "I thought I would surprise you."

"Where are we going?"

"That's my surprise." He flashed The Smile and leaned forward in the seat. "Take a turn at the next stop sign, right? You know The Lantern subdivision?"

Still, the driver didn't utter a word, nor did he turn to answer. He simply nodded. Leila said nothing. Instead, she placed her long fingers on Dan's thigh. With the other hand, she reached to pull his face closer…his lips to hers. Despite her gentle touch to his bruised cheek, he winced.

"You are going to tell me what happened, or no?" she said.

Suddenly, the taxi jerked to a stop. Indeed, they had reached the entrance to the cluster of suburbia called The Lanterns.

"Hang a right," Dan said.

The driver seemed unfazed by his direction, though he made a right turn as requested. Dan began to wonder if the guy was mute. Leila's hand was moving higher on his thigh now, not that he didn't enjoy the attention. He did. But this driver, he needed explicit directions.

They passed expansive, lavish ranch-style homes, constructed of brick sometime in the 1970's. Most had blazing porch lights framing the enameled front doors, which sat a considerable distance from the street. Mature oak and maple trees dotted the yards. Ah, here we are, the Hunter residence.

"Stop here, please," he said. When the car continued to roll, Dan slapped the gray vinyl that covered the backseat. "Stop!" What was going on with this guy? He wondered if he was ever going to turn around, or for goodness sake, talk! Dan stole a glance at the clock on the grimy dashboard—seven o'clock. Good. Bunny should be at the hospital by now, or the gym, or wherever she said she was going. He couldn't remember and he didn't care. He snatched a twenty from his thin wallet and offered it to the driver. "Keep the change," he said.

Actually, he wasn't sure how much the fare had been. He knew one thing. That twenty was the last of his cash. He would have to ask Bunny or Giles for more money. Well, he wouldn't worry about that now. Without a word, the driver sped away, and briefly, Dan realized something else. Somehow, someway, that guy looked familiar. Still, he couldn't place him. He was probably mistaken. Yeah, that was it.

"Why are we here?" Leila said.

They stood on the cracked sidewalk in front of Dan's house, directly in front of the long walk that led to the pastel pink front door. Well, it had been Bunny's idea, of course, and of course, Dan had said, 'of course.' He tried to put his arm around her, but Leila shoved him away with a shudder.

"Tell me just one thing," she said in a voice trembling with anger, "tell me this is not your house."

Dan's heart sank. Should he lie? Across the street, a porch light flicked on, while a dog barked, probably from boredom. He needed to get inside—fast—before someone saw him with Leila. She was, after all, famous, at least, in the social circles that surrounded Dan and the rich, radiant Dingwerths. His house? No, he decided. Another glance at the painted pink door told him what he needed to say.

"I'm getting a divorce, Leila. This is, you know, it's technically still my house, but that will be changing."

Big smile on her beautiful face, thank the moon and the stars above!

"You make me so happy," she said, hugging him.

He wanted to kiss her badly, so badly, but all he could think was, get up those steps and into that house before…

"Danny!"

Oh no! Leila jumped away from him. There were only three people in the world that called him Danny, like that. Of course, there was Bunny, but then, there were those two friends of hers—what did she call them—Puffy, Catty? In a flash, he wondered, did any of the people in Bunny's life have real names? Lo and behold, when he found the courage to turn around, he was indeed face to face with Bunny's Best Friends. Tonight was not his night.

"Hey, how are you?" was what he said.

Penny giggled. Candy giggled. What a surprise.

"We're fine," Penny said. "We were just on our way over to Ivymount to see Mrs. Dingwerth."

Great. Now they were staring at Leila. Even better.

"Do you know how she's doing?" Candy said. Her vacuous stare roamed the length of Leila's fabulous form.

"Who?" Dan said. His hands trembled. Would they tell Bunny they saw him with another woman? What would he tell Bunny? Candy giggled. Why were these girls laughing all the time?

"Bunny's mama, silly," Candy said. At the mention of Bunny's name, Dan sensed Leila's panic.

"Actually, Catty..." he said.

"It's Candy."

Ouch. Candy glared at him, in the same way that Bunny did whenever he was going to "pay" for a mistake. Better patch things up, fast. "Candy. What was I thinking? I'm just a little tired, I'm so sorry for the slip. It's just that I thought June was going home earlier today." Dan didn't like the frown on Penny's freckled face.

"Really? I could have sworn Bunny said she'd be visiting her at the hospital tonight." She paused, while she stared at the Hunter home, directly behind Dan and Leila. "Maybe Bunny's at home tonight," was what she said.

"Oh no, she's not," Dan said, perhaps a little too quickly, from the amused looks on the girls' faces. "I mean, I think she's over at her mother's house now."

"Uh-uh," Penny said. "Well, in that case, maybe we won't bug them."

"Right," Candy said. She gawked at Leila. "Hey, aren't you the model on the cover of this month's Cosmo?"

"So, you think maybe I look like her, eh?" Leila grinned, and for a moment, Dan thought she looked like a cat that just swallowed a goldfish.

"Absolutely."

Again, Penny giggled. "Candy, don't be so silly. What would a model want with Danny? Besides, Danny's got Bunny. What would he want with a model?"

Candy looked genuinely confused. "What did you just say?"

"We've got to be going Danny," Penny said. "Maybe next time you'll introduce us to your friend." She focused on the empty street ahead of her and started the engine. "Or not. Bye-bye."

"Bye," was all Dan could say.

What a disaster that meeting had been. If he was Leila, he thought, he would never speak to him again. Her resentful tone didn't surprise him. The spark in her dark eyes flared with her temper. "This was your idea of entertainment, no? The friends, they didn't say anything about a divorce. Not that I care if you do or don't."

"So why are you angry?"

"I care if you lie to me."

Dan checked his watch. 7:20. He wondered what Rocco was doing, or more specifically, Rocco and his Mercedes. Leila left him no time to think.

"Are you going to leave me out here on the sidewalk for entertainment too, eh?"

"I was thinking we should go back to your hotel room. This was a terrible idea. It didn't work out the way I thought it would, and Lei—"

Leila's mouth was on his. Her soft, moist lips tasted like sweet cinnamon candy. Dan felt breathless, even as he tried to speak. "Not out here, Leila. Let's get a taxi. We'll go back to your hotel."

"No! I can't wait for all of that, Dan. Not now. Now, I'll have to see the rest of your house, *mi amor*."

Right, thought Dan. There was still time. Bunny wouldn't be back for at least another hour, maybe two. He fumbled for his house keys. The truth was, he couldn't wait either. How they reached the front door, how they got inside; these things blurred in his mind. With Leila, time stopped. The world belonged to them.

Dan couldn't explain it, he didn't understand it, but he knew one thing: he was addicted to Leila Bolivar. He needed this habit. If a cure existed, it didn't matter. He didn't want any part of it.

Twelve

From Dan's point of view, one thing seemed strange—fortuitous, but very strange. Leila didn't want to share the bedroom he shared with Bunny. He didn't understand her decision, and she refused to discuss it. *Nada.* Perhaps the décor reviled her senses. After all, the pink walls, pink bedspread and cute accessories expressed Bunny's persona all too well. Perhaps its proximity to the front door attracted her to the guest bedroom. Certainly, it wasn't the 8x10 glossy of June Senior that held court on the solid maple dresser, the one in which June gaily displayed her tiny, yellow teeth. Whatever the reason, he felt no guilt whatsoever for whatever they were about to do, and for that, he felt grateful.

"Nice house, *mi vida,*" Leila said. She studied him over her shoulder while she removed her long black leather coat.

Dan waited in the doorway with an open bottle of wine and two wine glasses. "What did you call me?"

"*Mi vida.* It means, my life, my love. In Spanish, it's a term of endearment."

"You know, I know we haven't known each other that long, and yet, I feel like you know me better than anyone."

Leila unfastened her green silk blouse. She posed in the shadows, her naked body trembling in anticipation. Now, she turned to face him. "Dan, put down the wine. Please, the glasses, too."

Green silk, shadows, stardust and Leila—the cocktail entranced him. He set the bottle and glasses on the dresser in front of June's picture.

When he reached to turn out the bedside lamp, Leila stopped him. "No, *mi amor*, I want to see you."

He loved that about her. Bunny, however, insisted on the dark. She liked it that way, she said, the same way every time, in the dark.

With Leila, the possibilities seemed endless. For one thing, she flaunted her body. Though she was older than Bunny, he guessed by at least seven years or so, she used her body to tell Dan she wanted him. She would grab his hand and run it along the length and curves of her body, watching his face. And when they became one, Dan just knew-he belonged with Leila forever. If only they had met sooner, before Carlos, before Bunny, before…

The phone rang.

Leila's shoulders startled at the sudden jangle. "Don't answer it." Her wet tongue caressed his neck.

Certainly, he didn't want to, but something in June's smiling portrait called to him. What if something had really happened to her this time? "I have to." He reached across her breasts for the receiver.

"No, you don't," she said. Her long fingers caressed his thighs and then…

"Oh yeah, hi Bunny," he said, struggling to catch his breath. *What did Bunny want, right now, at this most inconvenient moment?* "No, I'm fine. How are you? Look, I said I'm fine. Oh. She's not? No Bunny. I won't be mad. You should do that. Bunny, I don't… Hi there, Giles. Yeah, sorry to hear about June." Suddenly, Leila's hand seemed frozen there. Was it his imagination? Had the temperature in the room just dropped twenty degrees? "No, I'll be in to work tomorrow. You can count on me, Giles. Bye."

Dan hesitated for a moment, while Leila stared at the picture on the dresser. June in her forties, he supposed. She really hadn't changed much, though Dan guessed she was somewhere in her sixties. Had she always looked so old? He reached for Leila's chin; he tried to stroke her smooth cheek. She brushed his hand from her face. Something changed between them. What happened?

"Who is Giles?" Leila's eyes never wavered from his bruised face. The clock in the hall chimed twelve times.

"Why?"

Leila sat up, and confronted him with folded arms. "I want to know. I want to know everything about you."

"Well, it's not very intriguing, but here goes. Giles is my wife's father."

"What? What does he look like?"

"Hey, I thought you were interested in me." Dan chuckled at his own joke. Leila did not. He noticed that and wondered. "Leila, what is wrong with you tonight?"

"Tell me what he looks like, damn it."

"Well, let's see. How do I describe Giles Dingwerth?"

"Dingwerth!"

"Yes Leila, I'm married to Bunny Dingwerth, I work for Dingwerth Distinctive Designs, and Giles Dingwerth IV is my father-in-law. Giles is about 6'1" tall, with white hair, and dark brown eyes. Sort of tan skin, even in the winter, don't know how the old boy does it. June is Bunny's mother, who by the way, is in a coma, and by the way, that's her portrait over there on the dresser. God knows she still looks the same as she did back then. Creepy stuff, huh? So, there you have it. Now, you know everything there is to know, except I guess what it is I do for Giles at Dingwerth Distinctive Designs. So, I'll tell you that part, too. I'm Vice-President."

For a second, Leila seemed distracted from her hysteria. "I'm impressed. What are you in charge of exactly?"

Dan stumbled for a second. His mind scanned his resume for an impressive credential. *Nada.* "It changes all the time. That's what makes my job so, so…"

"General?"

"No. I'm always in charge of something. Giles sees to that. Like tomorrow, for example, he can't be there for an important interview, so he makes sure that I am. Why are you so quiet all of a sudden? Are you mad about something?"

Leila buried her head in her hands. She sat cross-legged with her elbows resting on her knees. If he didn't know better, he would have thought someone had just died. She shook her head from side to side while she spoke. "I must tell you something. I want you to listen very closely. Nothing I say is going to change how I feel about you."

"Leila, I promise you, I'm getting a divorce."

Leila put her fingers to her mouth. "Shh. I've never felt about anyone what I feel for you. Not Carlos, not Roberto, not Diego, not Sergio, not—"

"You can stop now."

"Okay. It doesn't matter to me if you get a divorce or not. I don't care. I will love you, married or no." She shrugged and tossed her long, dark hair. "I feel if two people love each other, they should love each other. Life is short, you know?" She leaned toward Dan and kissed him, softly at first, with her eyes wide open; then, with her eyes closed, they share one long, passionate kiss. "I love you, Daniel Hunter, and I don't want anything ever to come between us."

"It won't, I promise. Why are you talking like this?"

Again, Leila stared at June's portrait. She took a deep breath. "Dan, I know Giles Dingwerth."

"So does half of this town, maybe all of it. What are you trying to say?"

"I'm saying, I *know* him. Intimately, like I know you, I know him."

"You mean, *know him*, like you've been with him?"

"Yes." Leila's voice sounded low and shaky.

"That's impossible. We can't be talking about the same guy."

"Does he like marmalade on his toast? Does he like his mashed potatoes with lots of gravy?"

"Well, yes, but—"

"Does the end of his mouth twitch when he's upset?"

"Yeah," he said, in a puzzled tone. "Does he have a driver who drives him around in a black Mercedes?"

It had to be Giles. Dan didn't see any point in answering Leila's last question. He didn't feel angry—just incredulous. It couldn't be, and yet, it had to be. Well, so what? He wasn't going anywhere. Leila was right. If they loved each other, then no matter what the price, they should be together.

"Dan?"

"Hmmm?"

"There's just one thing." Leila rubbed the back of her neck. Every word sounded heavy and labored. "His wife is very sick, no?"

"That's what they say. What are you getting at?"

"Will she die, do you think? Giles would be a free man."

Dan hadn't thought about much, actually. He hated to admit it, but he was beginning to see Leila's point. If June should die, Giles would be free, and these days, Dan did not enjoy that privilege. If Bunny had her way, Dan would be saddled with Bunny and Bunny Baby, while Giles and Leila…he didn't want to even remotely entertain the painful scenario.

"No, June won't die. This happens all the time. June just doesn't take care of herself, and her diabetes goes wacko. I've seen it happen before; it will happen again. Nothing to be alarmed about, trust me."

Bunny said she would spend the night at the hospital, did Danny mind too terribly much? For once, Bunny had perfect timing. Dan lay beside Leila that night, unable to close his eyes. Clearly, Leila trusted him, for she slept soundly. He only wished he could take his own advice.

After this bizarre discovery, he didn't know if he could go into the office tomorrow morning. What were the chances of such a coincidence? A cold chill ran down his neck. Giles had mentioned an interview with the Knowes woman tomorrow morning, hadn't he? That reporter must know about Leila! That's what she wanted to talk about-he just knew it. His gaze fell on June's photo. For the first time, he wondered about his mother-in-law and Giles. Did June know about Leila?

❖

The following day...

Gabby felt livid. For the second time in 3 weeks, Giles Dingwerth broke an appointment with her. Worse, he didn't even have the decency to reschedule, oh no. What did he do? He booked the fool who sliced her donuts into bullets to do the "up close and personal" interview. Would her readers forgive her? Ha!

When she spotted him, with his face all bruised up like that, she almost ran the other way. Then, she reconsidered. In her devious mind, he owed her an interview. With a juicy scoop, he could possibly redeem himself. Besides, he might give her some good gossip about his spoiled rotten wife, Bunnywitch that she was. Ooh, he was walking her way now.

"Hello Miss uh…" His eyes darted around the room as if he might find her name written somewhere on the stark white walls.

"Knowes. It's Gabby Knowes, from the Gateway Gabette. Do you recall the night of your car accident? I called 911 for you. Or, I've got it. Maybe you remember the first time we met, you know, the day you smashed a box of Krispy Kremes into the revolving door at the Hotel Charlotte. Any bells ringing in that head of yours? Ding-a-ling?" Okay, maybe she'd been extreme. Dan's reluctance to take a seat behind the massive mahogany desk told her that much. He stood by the closed door, his arms folded tightly across his trim body. For a moment, Gabby thought he would turn and leave. She thought wrong.

"Have a seat, won't you Miss Knowes?" he said, pointing to the burgundy leather sofa in Giles' office. Morning sunlight streamed through the airtight glass, revealing a fine coat of dust on the coffee table in front of the sofa. "Make yourself at home." He took a seat behind Giles' desk, staring and grinning in apparent amusement.

Gabby did not look amused. "You must know why I'm here today," she said, crossing her long legs.

Dan leaned back in the oversized executive leather chair. "Tell me."

"Well, by now of course, you must have heard the rumors."

"Rumors? About me?"

Gabby laughed. This guy had to be kidding or pathological-ly obtuse. "We'll get to those later. You can bet on that. No, I'm talking about those wild stories about Giles Dingwerth and that drop-dead gorgeous model. You know, the one from Venezuela? Caracas, I think it is. Everyone knows who she is, Mr. Hunter." Was she imagining things, or did she just see a quiver in Dan's shoulders? Maybe it was a sudden chill, but she wasn't feeling one. Nope, she was definitely feeling warmer.

Without hesitation, Dan replied. "You know, it's too bad that my father-in-law isn't here to defend himself, isn't it? I mean, I can't explain those types of crazy stories, especially with my mother-in-law in a coma over at Ivymount Medical Center. Don't you feel just a little disrespectful, Miss Knowes?"

Like a ravenous cat with a cornered mouse, Gabby consid-ered Dan. Any way she looked at it, she had Mr. Hunter where she wanted him. The real question remained, exactly where did she want to put him?

"Well," she began, recrossing her shapely legs, "I just thought your father-in-law might appreciate the chance to set the record straight, so to speak. As a conscientious reporter, I feel I owe the naked truth to my readers. Care to comment?"

Dan folded his hands on the desktop and glared at her with determination. "No. You can quote me on that."

Gabby uncrossed her legs. "Okay."

"Okay, then I assume we're finished here?"

"Oh noo-o. I'm just beginning."

"No, I don't think you are. In fact, I think one call to security should help you to wrap this up." Dan reached for the elaborate phone system, complete with fifteen lines to only-Giles-Knew-Where.

"I wouldn't do that just yet," Gabby said. "You do realize, of course, that you're confirming my suspicions? But hey, go ahead."

Dan set down the receiver. "What suspicions?" he said.

Gabby took a stab in the dark. "Well, you were seen at the

Hotel Charlotte two nights ago. Now, don't think I believe such a thing, but you might as well know it's out there. Rumor has it that you didn't leave until well after midnight," and-here, Gabby dropped her voice to a whisper—"that you were in Room 1204 the whole time. Care to comment?"

"You're a real troublemaker, aren't you?"

"Great minds think alike, don't they?" Gabby said, with a twinkle in her eye.

Dan rose from the chair, his jaw locked in rage. From the look on his face, the rumors about him and Mrs. Bolivar had to be true, Gabby concluded, at least in part. Now, he reached for her elbow to pry her from the sofa. "It's time you left the building."

"I only speak the truth. Don't you want my readers to know the truth?" Gabby planted her high-heeled shoes into the plush Oriental rug. Clearly, she did not intend to leave. Still, his hand gripped her arm insistently.

"I said, leave, and I meant it," Dan said. "If you choose to pick such a trying time in Dingwerth family history to print your trashy rumors, you will hear from our lawyers. I am very prepared to call security. Now, go!" His fingers clenched the flesh on her arm as he hoisted her to her feet.

She struggled to free herself and collapsed on the sofa. "I'm not leaving until..." Gabby's voice melted to a whisper, for there in the doorway, stood Bunny Dingwerth.

Now, she pointed at Gabby. "I knew something was going on. I'm telling you, woman to woman, sister, get lost!" Her hands were on her hips, her white plastic sunglasses perched on her cute nose, and her ponytail bobbed while she yipped and yapped, like a toy poodle that had been clipped a little too close to the skin. Her powder pink sweatsuit looked wrinkled and tired. Somehow, her white framed sunglasses had become awry and crooked on her cute nose.

Gabby was tempted, she really was. How could Bunny have known what Dan knew about Giles and Leila? If only she had. How could Bunny have known Dan feared Gabby would tell Bunny everything she knew? If only she had. Perhaps then, Bunny wouldn't have made such a fool of herself.

"I heard you came to harass my husband today. Daddy said Danny could handle whatever problems you threw at him. You ought to be ashamed of yourself, you know that? As if Daddy doesn't have enough on his mind, with Mommy still at Ivymount. And I know how upset Danny is too, even though he tries to hide it so he won't upset me. He's just too sweet, that's his problem."

"How is June?" Dan said, hoping to change the subject, as soon as possible, please and thank you.

"Who?"

"Your mother, Bunny. How is she?"

"Oh, she's much better. Dr. Hart says she can come home today at five. She needs her car. I hope you've been taking good care of it for her."

Gabby saw the panicked look on Dan's face. She didn't know if Bunny had or not, because Bunny prattled on and on about how Penny and Candy dropped by Mommy's hospital room today. Didn't Danny think those two were just the best friends ever? His face had suddenly gone very pale. What, Gabby wondered, was on Dan's mind?

"Danny," Bunny said, nudging the sunglasses high on her nose, "I didn't see Mommy's car in the parking lot when I showed up today. Where did you park it?"

"Hmmm?" Dan said.

"You know," Gabby said, "I've got to go now. Deadlines to meet and all that stuff, but then, Mr. Hunter here knows all about pressure, don't you, Mr. Vice-President of…I'm sorry, what is it that you're in charge of, sir?"

"Something. Danny's in charge of Something," Bunny said. "You can quote me on that, 'kay? Now, I hope this time you've got all you need. That way, you won't have to come back."

Amused and oddly relieved, Gabby eased her way past a tense Dan, a fuming Bunny, and into the noonday sunshine. Yes, she had all she needed, at least for now.

But, she would need to come back for more—much more.

Thirteen

Dr. Hart felt exhausted. This entire week had been simply exasperating, with Giles and his daughter Bitty, and worst of all, the late night phone call from Marc. Add to all of that the mediocre existence he led in that moldy apartment and well, one got the picture. He'd wanted, indeed needed, the divorce from Angela, no doubt about that. In fact, as he parked his silver Cadillac—finally!—in the hospital parking lot that morning, he actually struggled to recall whose idea it had been to initiate it. Things had gotten that bad.

Still, the call from Marc nagged at him for at least two reasons. The first one had to do with the sneaky suspicion that Marc felt a physical attraction to him. He'd only encountered it once before, back in medical school, when another student named—oh, what was his name—Alfie Hornsby, that's right, when Alfie put his hand on his knee during a film on heroin addiction. Funny, he still remembered it and he hadn't thought of it since, until today.

He didn't know what to do about Marc. Quite simply, he liked Marc as a friend, because he was a genuinely nice person, but that was all there was to it. His personal taste for more erotic pleasures had always run to the female persuasion. But, because of Marc's job at the Hotel Charlotte, he told Dr. Hart things from time to time that kept him "in the know," so to speak.

In short, Marc idealized Dr. Hart and Dr. Hart genuinely liked Marc. But, he wondered if the day would come when he would have to stop seeing Marc because the friendship had grown too intense. Because he would lose both a valuable friendship and breaking news on social scene, he sincerely hoped not.

His professional opinion of Giles Dingwerth loomed in the forefront of his mind. The irritating phone call with his soon to be ex-wife Angela, now coincidentally with Marc's ex-lover Brock, confirmed the rumors swirling in the dirty wind about Leila and Giles. Strolling up the stone walk to Ivymount Medical Center, his last conversation with June Dingwerth reverberated in his weary brain. *It's the model Leila Bolivar Giles wants, not me...If I should suddenly die, doctor, it might not be an accident.* Dr. Hart punched the elevator button. Were those the musings of a delusional diabetic, or the harsh truth? They could be either, or both.

He stepped off the elevator and into the stark wide corridor. Judging from the collection of jumbled trays stacked high on metal carts, breakfast had just ended. There was a steamy, sick bed odor hanging in the stale air. It never failed to amaze him that anyone recovered in such an atmosphere. Oh, there was Giles now, talking on his cell phone. Dr. Hart knew he shouldn't eavesdrop, but under the questionable circumstances...

"Leila darling," he heard Giles say in a muffled voice, "what is going on here? Don't tell me *nothing*. You never have time for me anymore. Well, it certainly doesn't seem like it. You know, I came by your hotel room last night, and by gosh, you weren't there. My wife? Oh dear, she was still in one of her comas, but she's fine as fish now." He must have felt Dr. Hart's stare, because he turned and said, "Oh dear, it's the doctor wanting to see me now. Got to go, darling. I'll call you."

Dr. Hart approached him, June's medical chart cradled in his right arm. "Well Giles, today's the big day, eh?" He managed a broad smile, searching for something in Giles' expression to speak to him, to tell him what he needed to know.

"What do you mean, Eugene?" The trap awaited.

"I mean, today is June's homecoming. She's made it through another coma. What a relief, right?" said Dr. Hart. *Talk to me, Giles.* But, Giles was not a stupid man. Dr. Hart sensed his defensive façade. The two men locked eyes for a second or two before Giles finally spoke.

"What else? Of course it's a relief. Why, I wouldn't know what to do without June. The question is Eugene, how much longer can the little Junebug go on like this?"

There is the answer. Bingo. Keep him talking. "I'm not sure what you mean." He tapped his pen on the chart, and waited. Giles selected his words carefully, he sensed that.

"I mean, what do you think? What is your medical opinion? Two weeks? Three months or six?"

Dr. Hart shook his round head. "It's impossible to say. Really impossible. June's a tough lady, we both know that. These things, these spells she has, they can go on for years, and why not? Between the two of us, she has the best medical care money can buy. Right, old boy? Giles? Is something wrong?" As if Dr. Hart needed to ask. He knew what the downcast expression on Giles's face meant. He'd said what Giles didn't want to hear, but therein lay the dilemma.

Dr. Hart had just heard the same thing.

"You know, Bunny," Dan said, while he stared at the white plastic sunglasses perched on Bunny's cute nose, "you really don't need those in here. There's no sunlight in my office."

"Don't tell me what I need. What I need is a car. Where exactly did you park Mommy's car?"

"Forget that. How did you get over here?"

"Penny and Candy stopped by Mommy's room on their way over to play tennis at the club. They gave me a ride over here. And you know what they said? They said they saw you the other night. Is that right, Danny?"

Uh-oh. A wave of chills rippled through his body. What was he going to say?

"Danny? Did you hear me?"

"Are they sure it was me?"

Bunny's forehead crinkled in confusion. "Well, they seemed

like it. The only thing was, they said you were with a lady with dark skin, and…we don't know anybody like that, do we Danny? Everybody we know has white skin, just like us." She snapped her fingers. "So you know what? They must be wrong." She giggled. "You know, I was kind of mad at you when I walked in, but I'm not anymore. How could I think that you would want anybody but someone just like me? I mean, ohmyGod, we have just the perfect life. Except, we still need a baby. Why don't we go have lunch and take a walk in the park? Danny, what's wrong?"

"There was something wrong with your mother's car and I had to leave it at the garage so they could fix it. I'm sorry I had to use your car to come in to the office today. I was afraid you'd be angry."

Bunny threw her arms around his neck and squeezed him. "Nothing you could do would make me angry. Let's go home, okay? I haven't even eaten my Lucky Charms today. Do you mind bringing the car to the front door?" she said with a giggle.

Dan grabbed the keys from Giles' top desk drawer. No, he didn't mind doing anything Bunny asked.

Not as long as he could see Leila for the rest of his life.

The rain drenched the sidewalk, while Bunny waited by the Dingwerth Distinctive Designs for Danny to pull up beside the curb. Something felt wrong between them, she was sure of it. For one thing, she hadn't seen The Smile for, let's see—she tried counting on her pink frosted fingernails, but lost track—well, it was just a very long time. He must be worried about Mommy, and on top of everything else, his car was in the shop. That was it! Here he comes now.

Bunny tried to cover her head with her pink clutch purse, but her golden blond hair was drenched by the torrents. Good thing she had her sunglasses to cover her eyes. She hated it when her mascara ran. What was that funny smell in her car? She crinkled her cute nose. It almost smelled like perfume. But Danny didn't wear perfume, and neither did she.

"Danny, what—"

"Did I ever tell you how gorgeous you are when you're wet?"

Well, no he hadn't. But still…

"Listen, I'm going to go by to pick up your mother's car now. That way, you can just drive your car home."

Okay, thought Bunny. That sounded good, except… "Danny, how do you know Mommy's car will be fixed? I thought something was wrong with it."

"Hmmm? Oh something was, but it's in tip-top shape now."

"Why can't we drive home together?"

"I thought you said you were hungry. Aren't you hungry? I want to talk to Luther for awhile, okay? He's the guy that runs the garage. Wouldn't a nice bowl of Lucky Charms taste good about now?"

It would. It sooo would. "Well, when will you be home?"

"Hmmm? Oh, an hour or two. Just go ahead and eat without me. I'll drive your mother's car to your parents' house and walk home."

"But, I can pick you up."

Why didn't Danny want to be with her?

"The walk will do me good. Look, here we are. There's Luther now."

"But Danny," Bunny said, squinting through the dark lenses of her sunglasses, "he's…is he black?"

"Yes, he is."

Bunny watched Luther approach the car with a bottle of root beer in his hand. What was Danny thinking, leaving Mommy's car with a black man? And why would he want to talk to him? One thing she knew for certain. She wasn't going to stick around in the pouring rain while Danny schmoozed with a black man. Well, he needed to get Mommy's car for now. Later, she would talk to Danny about who he would talk to. She watched her husband cross the side street. He stopped beside a tiny booth and a short, stooped black man with grizzled hair emerged. Dan turned to wave at her and then, he was gone.

Bunny drove down the street toward a busy intersection, headed for home. The rain began to wane, and she took comfort in the sight of the familiar shops and boutiques that lined the streets. Bunny liked shopping. She would have stopped if she were dressed in a cuter outfit.

Of course, she still needed to eat a bowl of Lucky Charms. And, she had a hair appointment with Brock Edwards in an hour, for a cut and color. Everybody said he was just the best stylist, even Penny, and that was saying a lot. She might have barely enough time to dash in and eat, and maybe change her clothes, she just didn't know. She had so much to do! It just didn't leave a girl much time to think about really serious things.

Serious things, like what her husband might be doing right about now.

Dan watched his wife's car disappear in the distance and sighed. It was a sigh of relief. Now, he would be free to spend a little time with Leila. He'd felt badly that he'd had to drop her off in such a tearing hurry this morning, after the torrid night they'd spent together.

"Hey man, I was wondering what happened to you." He turned to see Luther grinning at him. "None of my business now, but who's the pretty lady with the blond hair?"

Should he tell him? Why not? "My wife," Dan simply said.

"She's a pretty lady, man. Very nice. Why'd she drop you off?"

"Full of questions today, aren't you? Listen, things okay with that car I left with you the other day?"

"Sure."

Luther sucked a long swig from the amber bottle. Dan thought he saw a flicker of confusion in his dark eyes.

"Mind if I keep it here another hour or so? I've got a little business to do over at the Hotel Charlotte, and then, I'll pick it up when I'm finished. You don't mind, do you?"

"Mind? Naw."

A tense silence lapsed.

"Good. I'll be going then." Dan glanced up at the sky. "Looks like things are finally clearing up. The storm is over."

Luther strode off into the distance. "Maybe," was all he said.

Dan shrugged and strolled towards the Hotel Charlotte. He knew Luther saw him. He made another mistake.

He didn't wonder why.

Fourteen

Leila soaked in a warm bubble bath. Her long, dark hair hung in a loose knot at the nape of her swan-like neck. Salsa music played softly from her tape player, and still, she felt tense—tense and furious. Why? Why? Because Daniel had tossed her, yes, tossed her out by the curb this morning like, yes, a sack of potatoes, or a—a head of cabbage.

Who did he think he had here? She could have anyone she wanted—indeed, she always had. She didn't have to put up with him. She splashed her face with warm, soapy water and tasted the salty tears that dribbled down her high cheekbones. The tears fueled her anger. Daniel wasn't worth them.

She hardly knew him, and yet, he made her feel like no other man ever had. She had had flings with other married men, and she was, after all, a married woman. This one was different from the rest. This one made her want to leave Carlos. This one she wanted to keep for herself.

But, it made no sense, no sense at all. He was younger, and less sophisticated than her, with much less money than Giles could offer, but when he smiled—oh! She leaned back and closed her eyes, relishing the thought... Was someone knocking on the door?

There it was again. She wasn't expecting anyone. Well, she needed to get dressed anyway. She stepped out of the foamy water and onto the fluffy white rug.

"Leila!" she heard a voice in a half-whisper. "It's Dan, hot stuff. Open up."

Daniel? The nerve he had. She wouldn't see him. She would come to the door, but she wouldn't see him. She wrapped an oversized white towel, monogrammed with a large "C" in navy thread for "Charlotte," and tiptoed across the plush carpet. "What do you want?" Hurt and rage spiked her voice, and most of all, dammit, she wanted an apology. No, she told herself, she never wanted to see him again. No, she wanted an apology. No, she—

"Leila, I'm so sorry," Dan said in a muffled whisper. "Please, open the door."

She stood there, dripping rivulets onto the carpet that she thought she had missed in her hasty trip from the tub. She tasted the salt in the tiny droplets that dribbled on her cheeks—they were tears. Tears! She hadn't cried like this since, since.... The doorknob jiggled in insistence.

"Leila, please."

She couldn't open the door. She just couldn't. She stood and wept until the knob ceased to move. What if he left forever? What if she never saw Daniel Hunter again? Could she live with that? She wiped her tears with the edge of the towel. Yes, yes of course she could.

Yes.

No! She grabbed the knob and twisted. The door cracked. Leila was staring into a dim, empty hallway. Her heart plummeted like a leaden stone. Dan was gone. She craned her neck around the doorway, searching, searching...there he was.

"Daniel!"

Again, she began to sob. Now, her tears flowed like a gushing brook, her soul tasting the bitter wine of desire denied. She saw Dan running back to her, keys and coins jangling in his pockets, his face flushed with passion. Why was this moment so painful? Love was grand, wasn't it? Wasn't it?

Her pledge forgotten, she flung the door open wide. Dan rushed in, grabbing her body with both firm hands, the towel tumbling to the floor in abandon. His hands, *mi corazon!* Her heart desired him, with a driving, fiery passion that consumed her being. It didn't matter what else happened now or later.

Breathe—she must remember to breathe. She had gone some-place where time didn't exist; she was on a high that wouldn't end. Light, heat, wind, fire, all at once, she felt them. The minutes became half hours, then hours. She couldn't have said what happened if someone had asked her to recount the details. Indeed, when Dan woke her, she knew only contentment.

For the first time in her life, she felt "in love." Before Dan, before this moment, she'd never known such a feeling. But now, Dan would be the love of her life. Carlos would understand. She was sure of that, too. There was just one very big problem, of which she was also very sure—The Bunny. From what Dan had told her about his wife, Leila knew the Bunny would never understand. What, she asked Dan, were they going to do about his wife?

Dan lay on his back, staring at the ceiling. His demeanor was calm and his breathing was regular, which only made his declaration that much more outrageous. His expression barely changed, his eyes barely blinked when he spoke.

He answered as if he were planning a picnic in the park, or a visit to the zoo. Just a lighthearted way to spend an afternoon, eh? "We're going to kill her."

Leila sat up in bed and twisted her lush body toward him. Her skin felt clammy, and her stomach was queasy. What, she said without blinking, did he just say?

"Daniel, are you suggesting we murder The Bunny?" She couldn't believe his attitude. Was it arrogance? No, she didn't think so. She would call it confidence.

"I said," he said, taking her hands in his own, "we're going to kill her. It's the only way out. I've thought of everything, be-lieve me, and if we want to be together, we have no other choice."

"I don't understand. Why not a divorce?"

"I would lose everything I've worked for."

"But, you will anyway."

For a split second, he fell silent, silent and pensive. He rallied without hesitation. "Not if we don't get caught."

"We?"

"Okay, I. Or whoever does it. I've got a few people in mind."

"I don't understand."

"You don't need to. I'll take care of it. Just promise me one thing."

"Which is?"

"When this is over and Bunny is gone, we'll be together. Leila, promise me. I've never done anything this crazy in my life."

"Okay, we'll be together, but, I still don't understand. When will it be over? Tonight? Tomorrow? Daniel, why won't you look at me?"

"I can't tell you the details, that's why. No one must know, except me and—"

"Who?"

"Never mind. What are you going to do about Giles?"

"What about him? It's over, Daniel. I haven't told him exactly, but it is. I will miss his money, of course, yes, really miss it, but…"

Brrr-ing. The phone always seemed to know when not to ring—and rang.

Leila shivered. Suddenly, she felt very cold. "Hello," she said, staring at Dan. The steely determination on his face had replaced the flush of passion. Should she be flattered?

"Leila," said the voice on the other end, "it's Giles, darling. I'm down in the lobby and I thought I'd come up for a little visit, eh?"

"But I thought your wife was coming home from the hospital today."

"Oh, she is. And soon. That's why I don't have much time. I'm just so glad to find you in the room. Leila, is something wrong?"

"No, no. I'm just not ready for you, that's all."

"Don't worry about that. Besides, I have a little present for you."

Oooh. Leila loved presents, even if it was from Giles, and even if they were breaking up. After all, it was for her, wasn't it? She gestured to Daniel. "Okay Giles, you can come up now, but give me a few minutes, okay?"

Daniel shook his head, even as he proceeded to button his striped oxford shirt, pull on his khaki trousers, and slip on his trendy new loafers.

"Okay darling, bye," said Leila, replacing the receiver.

"Why did you tell him to come up here?" Dan's jaw looked taut with tension.

"Because I need to talk to him in person, remember? He is The Bunny's daddy, is he not?" Leila thought Dan looked a little paler than usual.

"Yes," he said, "I guess he is."

She felt his arms around her and again, she shivered. Again, she felt very cold, perhaps because his words chilled her in her bones.

"Leila, let me worry about Giles, about Bunny, about us, okay? You don't want to know anything more than I love you like I've never loved anyone before now, and I want to be with you always. It won't be long darling, and we'll be together forever."

The crisp, hard knock on the door shattered the moment. "Leila darling, it's me." The doorknob jiggled insistently. Leila felt frozen with panic, then fear.

"Let me get it," Dan said. A brooding anger clouded his handsome face.

"No, Daniel, are you crazy? You don't need to confront Giles. Get in the bathroom and shut the door. I'll talk to him and then, it will really be over."

For a second, she could tell, Daniel weighed the options. Finally, he dragged his feet into the bathroom and shut the door.

Giles pounded on another one. "Leila, for God's sake, open up! I don't care if you're ready or not."

Leila threw a red satin robe around her thin body and scurried to the door. Even she wondered, was she ready—or not? She put a smile on her model's face and opened the door.

Bunny noticed it the moment she opened her front door. It was that same spicy, pungent smell, the same one that still lingered in her car. Wasn't it? She thought it reminded her of cinnamon, maybe cloves, some spice that started with a *C*. Kind of like Dingwerth Distinctive Designs started with a *D*, she mused, something like that. She flipped on the light in the foyer and climbed the steps to the master bedroom.

Something was very wrong between Danny and her, she was now sure of that. She would have dearly loved to think that that Gobble Gobble reporter, or whatever her name was, was the entire cause of the strife, but, even as she hopped into the steaming shower and lathered her fluffy hair, she had a weight on her shoulders she couldn't explain. She reached for the bar of pink soap and instantly quit. Wait, what was that noise. It was the sound of something dropping, or was it? Was someone downstairs?

She checked the time on her watch: one thirty. If she really rushed, she would have just enough time to throw on one of her cute outfits and get to Brock's salon by two. She perked up her pink ears. Wait, there it was again. What was that sound? It sounded like scraping, metal against wood. Should she go downstairs?

Well silly, she chided herself, she had to go downstairs, because she had to go to Beauty by Brock. It had taken her two months to get this appointment and she wasn't about to cancel it just because she heard a scary noise. It was probably the furnace anyway, or something like that. Really, she couldn't stop to check it out at a time like this.

She snatched a leopard print jumpsuit from the walk-in closet and cinched the waist with a chain belt made of wide gold loops. A pair of golden slides completed her "look." Okay, she was off and out. She rushed through the kitchen on her way out, grabbing an apple from the fruit bowl on the counter. Sunshine streamed through the bay window, casting midday shadows on the oak cabinets. Skipping through the foyer on her way to the car, she couldn't help but notice that smell again. Spicy, that's what it was. Like chili. She smiled. That started with a *C* too.

Like the car that was parked across the street.

He kissed her full on the mouth, and he knew. Just like that. She had someone else. How did he know? Giles released her, at least from his embrace. If anyone knew what a fading love looked like, felt like, hurt like, well, he did. He'd inflicted that dying love on June long enough to recognize the symptoms of the disease, and now, he was becoming its hapless victim.

In fact, from the look of things, someone had been here not too long ago. Who, he wondered? Who had been here? He proceeded to walk to the wide window, almost brushing Leila to one side. Almost.

"What is it, Giles?" she said, trailing behind him. "Didn't you say you had something for me, darling?"

"Is that what I mean to you? Is it always about what new gift I might have for you, Leila? Aren't you even glad to see me?"

"You know I am, *mi amor.*"

Giles gazed out over the gleam of the silver Arch, the symbol of the Gateway to the West.

"Something's changed between us. I can feel it."

"No darling. No."

"Yes, sweetheart. I've been thinking. Not that it matters, but do you want to tell me who it is? It's not like you to not be ready for me in the afternoon. Look at you, you're not even dressed. Why would you ask me to wait a few minutes before coming up? You never have before today."

"Giles darling," Leila said, her eyes fixed on the closed bathroom door, "I just don't know why you're talking like this. Look at me." She took his face in her hands and kissed him.

"It's not you, it's just that…"

"Yes?"

"Maybe we've been spending too much time apart, or too much time together, or maybe, it's your wife."

"Of course it's my wife! Don't you see? If June had died, we could have been together forever, but no… She's goddamn immortal!" He shook his head. "She'll be home by five-thirty tonight."

"Don't you have to pick her up at the hospital?"

"Oh no, June wouldn't have it like that. She's coming home in an ambulance, no less. I'm telling you, Leila, a divorce would be devastating for me, but—tell me something—how do you manage with Carlos? Does he know about us?"

"Carlos and I understand that, from time to time, we may meet attractive people and life is short, is it not? We are, what do you call it—discreet. What is wrong?"

"I want you for myself. I thought you felt the same way about me."

"I enjoy your company, Giles, but you know, I am a married woman. I see no reason to change that. You are forgetting that you are a married man."

"If I wasn't?"

"But you are!"

Giles reached into his coat pocket and retrieved a tiny blue velveteen box. "Open it, Leila."

A puzzled expression crossed her face. There was really only one thing it could be, wasn't there? If she accepted an engagement ring, well… The brilliant five carat diamond solitaire glimmered like a chunk of white fire. She couldn't help herself. She put it on her ring finger, left hand.

"Do you like it?" Giles said.

"Like it? Like it? I love it. But, it looks like an engagement ring, and Giles, I…"

"It is an engagement ring. And, you accepted it." His plan was working. He knew it would. Perusing the room, he noticed the closed bathroom door. From the crack beneath, a ray of light blazed. "Leila, is there…" he began, but his focus shifted back to Leila's objections.

"You are married, and so am I."

"Then, there's only one thing for us to do, isn't there? You must decide, Leila."

"What about you?"

"I already have." He took her in his arms once more, and kissed her. Still, there was something missing. Giles was not a dim-witted man. He sensed the flame that had once simmered beneath their passion had cooled. Leila's kisses were well, routine, and Leila was not a routine woman. Someone, somewhere was garnering the kisses he craved. "I have to go now, but I'll call you tonight. Unless, you want to give the ring back to me."

At the suggestion, Leila covered the ring with her right hand. Giles grinned. "Aha. That's what I thought." He turned to leave.

The door slammed behind him.

Fifteen

Brock was running behind, again. As hard as he tried to stay on time with each one of his clients, it was impossible for him to rush someone out of his chair when that poor, distraught person was "venting," as Marc used to like to call it. Sometimes, he knew he was the confidante, and he just couldn't risk disappointment. Sometimes, a client asked and answered her own questions in the same breath. Such was the case with Angela's neighbor, Mrs. Claus.

Actually, she didn't have that much hair. Cottony and white, he fluffed and teased it every Friday without fail. Fragile and stooped, she sat hunched in the chair in a motionless pose while her mouth chattered. Now, she was telling him about her newest boyfriend. "Tell me the truth, Brock," she said in a hushed tone. "Is he too young for me?"

Before he could answer, she did. "Oh, I know what you're thinking, and you're wrong about him, dead wrong. I love what you did with my hair today, Brock. It looks so full and shiny, don't you think? Don't answer that, you're just so hard on yourself! You've just too modest, did you know that? Of course you did. Wish me luck on my weekend in Vegas!"

Brock rearranged his combs and scissors. According to his watch, it was now twenty minutes past two, and his new client, according to his appointment book, was one Bunny Hunter. Was it Miss or Mrs., he wondered?

"Mr. Beauty by Brock?" said a squeaky voice behind him.

He turned and pointed to himself. "I am Brock, yes."

Before him stood a tanned, toned, twenty something, double-processed bottle blonde, he supposed it was Scandinavian Sunset #9, clad in a leopard print jumpsuit. Could this be Bunny Hunter? His clammy palms and dry mouth told him it could, and yes indeed, that it was.

"And you must be Penny's friend. Love your look. It's so, *jungle.*"

"I am Bunny Dingwerth Hunter. My father owns Dingwerth Distinctive Designs. Have you heard of it?"

Brock swallowed hard. Her father was Giles Dingwerth? The name jogged a wicked memory. Well, so what if her father was a philandering tycoon?

"Please Mrs. Hunger, um, Hunter, please sit down in my chair. I so apologize for the wait. Mrs. Claus had a special weekend coming up and..."

The shrill peal of giggles startled him. "Her?" said Bunny. "A special weekend?"

"Why, yes. A new boyfriend, in Las Vegas!"

"You're too funny, you really are. Penny didn't tell me you were this funny."

Penny didn't tell me you were this petty, thought Brock. He combed his tapered fingers through her fine, thin hair. "So tell me, what are we doing today?"

"I want highlights, I think. Maybe like yours." Again, the giggles. "Or maybe I'll go red like Penny. It's just that I think my husband is bored with my look, and I thought I'd change my hair. That should fix everything, right?"

He would have to talk to Penny about this referral, he really would.

"I mean, you're a man," she rambled on, "what would fix things for you?"

Suddenly, she stopped and stared at him, wide-eyed as a child. "Oh God, you're not gay or anything, are you? I mean, a lot of hairdressers are, not that I actually know any or anything." She seemed to be holding her breath, waiting for an answer.

Brock's mouth smiled. "Don't worry about it." No, he wouldn't say a word to anyone, but Bunny's barb had made him feel, well, evil. "How about we try red with gold highlights?" he said with a wink. "Or, take it a step further. Picture blonde with red highlights." He stood behind Bunny and grinned, while she frowned into the mirror. "Well, what do you think?"

"I can't. I mean, can you just touch up my roots?"

Brock studied Bunny's reaction in the mirror. He saw her lips begin to tremble, and her eyes well with fresh tears. "Mrs. Hunter," he said, "why don't you just relax here in my chair, and we'll talk for a minute, okay? I make a luscious cup of tea, with a special lemon twist. Can I tempt you?" Her face brightened like the dawn. She smudged her eyes with a pink tissue. What an amazing transformation, thought Brock. It was simply amazing.

"Penny said you were just the best," said Bunny. "You're right, we should talk about this. Thanks, Brock. Please, call me Bunny."

Brock gazed at the blonde, tanned woman in his chair and suddenly, he saw something he hadn't seen. Beneath the cosmetic façade, beat the heart of a woman in fresh pain. Well, she'd come to the right place. Brock knew all about broken hearts.

Better get that tea.

The bathroom door burst open and Dan stormed out, his face contorted in rage. "Okay Leila, show me the ring," he said, his words clipped and short. "Don't you think that was a little callous? Just a little rude? You knew I'd hear every word."

"Daniel, please let me explain."

"No, I don't think so. Giles is right, you know." The diamond sparkled, even in the gloomy room. "You do need to decide." Hot, bitter tears streamed down his ruddy cheeks.

"But, I have. I want you."

"You have a funny way of showing it. You know something else? I need to go." He reached for the doorknob and twisted.

"Daniel! If you would just give me a chance…"

Without a word, Dan stepped into the dim hall. It smelled

of pine scent and French fries. He needed to think, he needed to breathe, but most of all, he needed to decide. In a frenzied huff, his hair mussed and his tie askew, he made his way to the lobby, home of the infamous revolving doors.

He never noticed the redheaded reporter gabbing with Marc at the marble reception desk—the one who checked her watch when he rushed off of the elevator—but, she noticed him. No, he was headed for Luther's Fine Parking. He would pay Luther's outrageous rate for his fine parking, get June's car back, and head over to the Dingwerth residence, where he would bet a box of Lucky Charms that Bunny was waiting for June Senior's homecoming. Oh boy.

Hey, there was Luther now, wiping down the windshield of a white Cadillac Escalade. So absorbed was he in his work, he never heard Dan's approach until he was almost directly behind him.

"Hey!" he finally said, stuffing the rag into the front pocket of his workshirt, "I was about to come looking for you."

"Me?" Dan shielded his weary eyes from the glare of the late afternoon sun with his hand. "Why? Don't tell me you lost my car."

"Naw, it's nothing like that. It's just that somebody came around about two o'clock today, looking all over for you."

"Me?"

"Yeah, you. Said Rocco from the club told him where he could find you today. So, he comes to talk to me. And, I'm telling you, I don't want no part of whatever this mess is, because of I don't like the kind of message he gave me to give you."

"Which is?"

Luther grabbed the keys to June's Cadillac from one of the many hooks on a plywood board hung on a dingy wall in his wooden shack. Dan didn't like the suspicious look on his face when he turned to answer him. This Luther was too shrewd, maybe too much for his own good. "Hope you know what he's talking 'bout, because I surely don't. Guy says there's a big problem with what you want him to do, something about a down payment or something. Says he don't do no deals—not the kind you looking for—without a little dough up front. You dig?"

Oooh boy. Rocco hadn't said anything about a down payment. "You say this wasn't Rocco?"

"No man, I know who Rocky is. Me and him had a sodie the other day. Wasn't him."

"So, what did he look like?"

Luther squinted into the distant horizon, as if he could find the person if he looked hard enough. "Let's see. He had brown hair. No, make that black, and brown eyes—I think they were brown—and he was about as tall as me and you. Yeah."

Which made him stand out like a blade of grass on a lawn, this description. One thing was for sure. Dan had asked Rocco about contract murder because he was pretty sure Rocco had some connections that way. An account of the time that one of Rocco's enemies mysteriously "disappeared" had told him that much. It hadn't been that long ago, either. Dan had every right to assume Rocco's connection was still in business for his business with Bunny, even if Luther, Bunny's notorious "black man," wanted nothing to do with the plan.

There, he'd admitted his guilt. Now though, he was so confused. Things weren't so clear after all. Yesterday, he'd have bet his future on Leila's feelings for him. She said she loved him, and besides, he could feel it in the torrid passion between them. Passion was love, wasn't it? Wasn't it?

All he knew was that he'd never felt this way before and probably never would again. At least, he couldn't imagine such a feeling twice in a lifetime. He had to seize the moment while he could, or spend the rest of his life wondering what could have been and living with Bunny, Bunny Baby, and June Senior, maybe even Giles, too. There was no contest. The die had been cast.

Once again, he had a Plan.

Dr. Hart sat at the nurse's station, reviewing June Dingwerth's most recent chart. He didn't even want to think about all of the others that lingered somewhere in the dark cavern known as

Medical Records. How long had June been his professional patient? He flipped through the pages, idly computing the years he'd known her. It was something like twenty or twenty-five, wasn't it? At least half of her married life. He reflected that it must be trying for old Giles, at times. Married life at best was trying at times, wasn't it?

No one knew that better than Dr. Hart.

Speaking of Angela, why was she calling his cell phone at this very moment? Hadn't he told her not to call him at work? Besides, his cell phone didn't work very well inside the dense concrete walls of the hospital. Still, he would answer it, anything to silence that annoying, nerve grating ringtone. "Hello Angela, yes it's me, how are you, I'm fine," he droned while he scrawled the word DISCHARGE across June's chart.

"So, what's on your mind? You sound, pardon me for saying so, but you sound so agitated. No, I'm not picking on you. I'm right, aren't I?"

He cradled the phone under his chin while he arranged the chart. "Oh, so that's it. Brock's late. Well, and why not? He runs—what did you say it was—a salon, that's right. It was probably an extra busy day, just like I'm having. That's right, like I'm having, the one that still pays your bills. Let's not get into this now. My lawyer will call your lawyer, that's right. Tell Brock good luck for me."

The more time he spent away from that woman, the more he felt the divorce was the right thing to do. Why then, did the sound of her voice still upset him so much? Because, he realized while strolling down the corridor to June's room, because in spite of everything—her infidelity, his occasional gambling problem, her compulsive shopping habit, his binge drinking—she was still the only woman he had ever truly loved. Now that he was about to be a free man once again, he wondered if that would ever change.

Ooops, there's June's room, the one that resembled a floral scented theater stage, featuring June Dingwerth as the main attraction. He paused just outside the room to straighten his tie, and was surprised to see a young, fine-looking man making his way down the hall. Funny thing, he didn't know June had a son, especially one with such a magnetic smile.

"Hi," said the young man, "I'm June's son-in-law, Dan Hunter. You know, Bunny's husband."

Dr. Hart didn't want to confess that June had never mentioned him. "Dr. Eugene Hart." He clasped Dan's sweaty palm in his smooth one. "I'm afraid you're a little late for a visit today. I was just getting ready to tell June she could go home."

"Really? I was hoping to have a few words with her." Dan flashed The Smile, the whitest smile that Dr. Hart had ever seen. The doctor was intrigued, but he needed to move on to his next patient. Besides, he did have another motive. He was meeting Marc for drinks at seven o'clock. "I won't be but a minute, I promise," he said. Dan tapped his foot.

"Neither will I," said the doctor. "I need a few moments with Mrs. Dingwerth, please. Alone, if you don't mind, please." *Anxious guy. Wonder if he's like that all of the time?* He rapped on June's door. There she was, propped up in bed, surrounded by flowers. If she'd been lying down, she might have been mistaken for an expensive corpse.

"Eugene," she said, "should I stay another day? What do you really think? Is it safe to go home, I mean, really safe?"

Dr. Hart took a deep breath. After all, he did not have a crystal ball. "June, how long have we known each other?"

"I'm sure I don't actually know. What's that got to do with anything?"

"Because I'm going to say something I've never said to any other patient of mine before, and frankly, I can't believe I'm saying it to you." He stared at the pale woman with the tiny yellow teeth. There was no turning back now.

"Do you recall what you said to me about, oh let's see, how did you put it? You said something like, if you should die suddenly, it might not be an accident. It might not be the way it was meant to be, or something like that. Do you remember that discussion?"

June had grown solemn. "Yes Eugene, but what..."

"Do you want to talk about that? Tell me why you said such things."

June looked away and her pointy chin jutted into the air. "I really can't remember why."

The doctor stared at her for a few moments. Should he or shouldn't he? Well, he wasn't a police officer was he? June Senior was a big girl now, all grown up. He wasn't her parole officer, after all. He signed the discharge papers. "Alright then June, you're a free woman. You know what I always say. Watch yourself, hmmm? Not too many sweets this time around. Oh, and your son-in-law is here to see you."

"Dan? Dan is here?"

"I think he said his name was Dan, yes. I really must go now. Call the office for an appointment, hmmm?" He was probably imagining his suspicions, thought Dr. Hart. It was just sheer craziness to suspect foul play in a prosperous, respectable family like the Dingwerths. Wasn't it?

He passed Dan on the way out and nodded. Seemed like a nice enough young man, but there again, no one had ever mentioned him, not that he could recall. Strange, wasn't it? Or, maybe it wasn't.

The plain fact was, he thought while he drove his car onto the highway, the Dingwerths were odd ducks. What was strange behavior for many people could seem perfectly normal for people like them, whatever people like them were like. Still, if his instincts were correct, and they usually were, his instincts screamed louder the farther away he drove. Something about fraud, something about deceit, something about money. Add them all up, and what did he get?

He pulled into the parking lot of the Green Parrot Lounge and leaned against the steering wheel. His stomach felt bloated, acid burned his throat. Answer the question, Hart, he chided himself. C'mon, what did he get? From the depths of his mind, June's words echoed, "...it might not be an accident. It might not happen in the way that it was meant to." Fraud + Deceit + Money = Accident?

Or not. He just didn't know anymore.

A visit from Dan? June couldn't figure this one out. This, or anything else, for that matter. Everyone, including Eugene Hart, had been acting as if she was going to die any minute, and that was simply out of the question as far as she was concerned. Oh, she'd had a little scare now and then, but who hadn't? Why was everyone so, so tense? Well, here was Dan, no time to think about all of it.

The late afternoon sun glared through the open blinds and Dan squinted, turning his head away from the wide window. "How are you, June?"

Odd. Very odd. She would get right to the point. "Dan, would you like to be the one to tell me what is going on?"

Dan plopped in the padded armchair beside her bed and closed his eyes, but only for a second. "I was hoping you could tell me."

"What do you mean?"

"What do *you* mean?"

"Dan, why did you come to visit me now? Did you know I was going home this evening?"

"I had heard that, yes, but…"

"Then why are you here? You obviously have something on your mind. Can't it wait until I get home?"

"No, it can't. Just hear me out. See, there's something you should know."

"About what?" This was like pulling teeth, thought June. Just listening was making her sick again, and yet, something about Dan reminded her so much of herself. What was it? Trapped. That's what he was saying; trapped, all these years, just like her. My God, was she losing her mind? All of these blasted narcotics were making her thinking so fuzzy today. Now, Dan was mumbling away again, his hands wringing themselves raw, something about—yes, she heard him correctly—trapped! He felt trapped!

"I've tried to talk to Bunny about this, but you're going to hate me, aren't you? Is Bunny coming here or is she waiting back at the house?"

"I don't understand. Or maybe I do, I just don't know. Did you have a fight with Bunny—is that it? Because Giles and I learned how to fight years ago, Dan. And now, we don't argue at all, anymore. Because, you see, we both just know how it is, you see."

Dan glanced up at her with a blotchy, tear-stained face. "How it is? What do you mean? How what is?"

"You know, as the years go by, you just learn what to expect. It all becomes predictable. You know what you're going to get from your relationship, and what you're not."

"See, there it is—what you just said—about what you're not going to get."

"What about it?"

"How do you ever get it?"

"Well, Dan, you don't. You just don't. That's life. You make choices, and that's all there is to it."

"June, are you happy?"

"I don't know. I should be. People tell me I should be, and so, I suppose I am. I set out to marry a wealthy, good-looking man, and I did, so I did what I set out to do. I should be happy about that."

Dan smiled, a sad, wistful smile. "You mean, you had a plan and you reached your goal, is that what you're saying?"

"Yes. That's exactly what I'm saying."

"June, do you believe in love at first sight?"

At this question, June's expression softened. For a moment, her tender memories carried her to a distant place and time. "I did. Maybe I still do. But, you know Dan, a love like that can break your heart. I wonder, is that a love worth having?" She paused and cleared her throat. "I did what I set out to do, and I should be happy about it. So, I am. Besides, what's the choice? It's far too late for me to choose anyone else." June frowned. Her gaze never wavered from Dan's face, even as she spoke, slowly, deliberately.

"And frankly, Dan," she said, "it's too late for you as well."

Dan kissed her on the cheek and left the room, satisfied he had the answer to his dilemma. Until he was alone again, to think about the possibility that June was right: that there was no such thing as magic, or angels, or miracles or love at first sight. Only carefully laid, rational plans that either worked or didn't. No magic in the moonlight for June, or he supposed, for him.

He pulled onto the highway; his frenzied mind whipped into a whirlwind of what-ifs. Dammit, he wasn't ready to die yet. Even if she vanished tomorrow, a moonlit magic had once upon a time enchanted him. Suddenly, he realized the tragic truth of June's reality.

Her rational plans had ensured her security, yes. Was not security the foe of stardust and miracles? She'd never sense the gust of wind beneath an angel's wings, or know the giddy intoxication of wild roses simmering beneath a summer sun. Scarlet passion would never scorch her heart; nor would her fondest dreams dissolve in a river of bitter tears. No passion or dreams for June. Ah, security!

Dan knew one thing. June had never known anyone like Leila Bolivar. Lately, however, the magic seemed to be fading; the twinkle in Leila's stardust had grown dull. Perhaps Rocco knew more about women like Leila than he did, Dan decided. *That's what he would do!* A beer or two with Rocco, and together, they would solve the mysteries of a woman's mind. Once again, Dan had a Plan.

Sixteen

Bunny took a long sip of the steaming tea. Her nose wriggled at the lemony scent. Her eyes looked pink and swollen from sobbing and a pile of scrunched pink tissues lay piled in her lap. "Are you this nice to all of your customers, Brock?"

"Of course I am. Feeling better?"

"Yes, but I haven't told you what's wrong yet."

"You haven't told me what we're doing to your hair, either." Brock grinned.

Bunny took another sip and wiggled her pretty pink nose. "The thing is, I don't know what to do. But, I do know one thing."

Brock leaned down close to her ear and whispered. "What is that?"

"I have to do something. Something really different."

"But really, you are quite attractive the way that you are, Mrs. Hunted. I mean, Hunter, uh...Bunny."

"I have it! I have an idea!"

Those were the words Brock dreaded most. In his thirty-two years of experience, they almost always meant trouble on the network. He had decided something else as well. He would have to think of a memorable way to thank Penny for this referral, he really would, because he wanted her to think twice before she ever did something like this a second time. For now, he had his work cut out for him. "What is that idea? You can tell me."

"Take me darker. Much darker. I mean, down to my natural col...oops."

Brock stared at the coffee-colored roots on Bunny's scalp, not yet an inch long. He couldn't believe a girl like Bunny really meant what she had just said. "Do you know what you are saying? It will alter your appearance completely. You will have to change your makeup, possibly even your choice of clothing, everything. You'll look like a totally different woman."

Bunny squealed with delight. "Oh goodie, goodie, goodie. Danny will be so surprised. Not to mention Mommy. Well, June— I mean June Dingwerth is her real name, did I tell you that?"

Brock had seen a lot of customers come and go throughout the years. Most wanted to enhance their appearance, some wanted simply to maintain it, and then, there were those like Bunny, who wanted to completely change it. In Brock's experience, this signified more than just an outward transformation. Hadn't she mentioned husband trouble? What was that about her Mommy, The June?

"Do you think your own mother will recognize you?" he said with a slight chuckle.

Suddenly, Bunny grew somber. "It might cheer her up. She's been so sad."

"Sad? Why?"

"Who really knows? She doesn't say much, and when she does, you'd swear she was delirious. Like the other day at the hospital, she was telling us that someone was trying to kill her."

"What did you just say?"

"I know. Have you ever heard of anything so ridiculous? She insisted she didn't want to go home because it wasn't safe. She said someone tried to poison her."

"What do you think?"

"I think it's crazy, and I'm sure Dr. Hart does too. The only people who live in the house are Daddy and Felicity, and well, it's plain crazy to think that they're trying to kill her. I mean, why would they want to do that?"

"Maybe she knows too much about something." From the look of despair on Bunny's face, he wished he hadn't said that last remark. From the look on Bunny's face, maybe she knew too much for her own good as well. He felt uneasy. It was time to simply do his work and call it a day. "Well, let's mix your hair color, shall we?"

Bunny clapped her pink hands in anticipation. "I'm just so excited. Hey Brock, maybe my husband will think I'm someone else. Wouldn't that be like, the ultimate compliment?"

Brock smiled and strolled back to the color room. He wouldn't have taken it that way. No, he wouldn't, but…maybe Bunny Hunter knew too much for her own good.

The Green Parrot Lounge would not have been Dr. Hart's first choice for a casual drink. Marc insisted it had a certain ambiance, and well, he did work at the Hotel Charlotte, after all. He was the expert on ambiance. Still, once the doctor parked in the lot littered with empty cans and bottles, he was afraid to get out of his car.

The gangs that dotted the dark parking lot intimidated him, not to mention the various "ladies" who lurked in the shadows. It had been seedy when Dr. Hart was last here with Angela, and that had easily been five years ago, but Marc had assured him the lounge had improved. *Ah, Angela.* How those memories still stung like a hornet. Somehow, he would have to find a way to move on without her.

He pulled his keys from the ignition and opened the car door. The frigid night air blasted his face, and he gasped. He hadn't expected the wind to be so harsh. Amid the figures loitering in the parking lot, he trudged to the front door of the lounge. He was amazed that, although he felt the wanton stares, he was not approached. Must be his devil-may-care attitude, he decided.

It was a good thing he'd saved his energy. The moment he opened the creaky front door, his solace ended. A gruff voice boomed from the corner near the end of the bar. "Who're you?"

Where was Marc? Was he in the right place? Never one for weapons before now, the doctor suddenly wished he possessed one. The customers slouched at the bar glanced at him with an inexplicable contempt. He was about to leave when he saw him: a short, wiry man in his thirties with a chip on his shoulder to match his surly swagger.

"Cain't you hear, boy?" he said. "I said, who're you?"

Dr. Hart felt the sticky silence. Everyone was staring at him. "I must be in the wrong place. Is this the Green Parrot Lounge?"

"What's it look like?"

Clearly, thought the doctor, he can't expect me to answer that question. How does one describe a place where women's undergarments hang from the blades of ceiling fans, and a hand-carved wooden sign by the bar reads, "No means no, and yes means maybe?" He was on the verge of leaving when he heard him.

"Eugene! Over here!"

Peering through the smoky haze, he saw him emerging from what seemed like a back room behind the bar. It was Marc, dressed in a geometric print shirt and silken gray trousers. Sleek and lean, he made his way to where he stood. "It's okay, Tugg. He's with me."

"With you? You're kiddin'."

"Get us a couple of drinks, okay?" He turned to the doctor. "What are you having?"

"Uh, whatever you are. Listen, Marc—"

"Just a couple of Bud Lights. We'll be over here." Marc gestured to a corner table. "This okay with you, Eugene?"

"Marc, I don't know about this place. I mean, why—"

"I thought you might ask. It's an unlikely choice for me, I know that. But, here I can be what I want, with who I want."

Dr. Hart twitched with nervous tension. "You're kidding."

"I suppose I didn't explain the reason."

"Which is?"

"The Green Parrot Lounge is an investment for me. Kind of like a retirement nest egg. You should have seen this place when I bought it last year. It's really come a long way."

"You're kidding."

"Would somebody say something new? Please, I'm not

kidding. I mean, I'm perfectly serious about this place, and no one ever seems to believe me. It was condemned a year ago, and look at it now. Okay, maybe business isn't exactly booming yet, but I'm breaking even most months, and around holiday time, things really start to pick up. The only thing that hasn't improved much are my employees' manners, and okay, maybe their hygiene could use a little work. The Health Department had a little talk with me about that one. Okay, I'll admit some minor issues, but there's room for improvement in any business, right? I talk to my people from time to time, and things do improve around here—for a little while. See, the way I see it, a guy has to have a plan. He has to have goals."

Marc paused for a moment while Tugg grudgingly slid two beer bottles across the wooden table. He nodded at Tugg and continued. "Which brings me to the reason I asked you to meet me here tonight."

"You've got me on the edge of my seat, you really do. Don't tell me you want me to invest my money in this place." He stared at the beer in front of him, too intimidated to make eye contact with the other customers.

"Forget it, Eugene. This place is all mine, buddy. No, actually, this is something that already involves you."

"Me? What is it?"

"I believe we have a mutual, uh, friend? Well, maybe that's not the right term. Acquaintance might be more like it."

"You're driving me crazy with all these innuendos. What is this, a game of cat and mouse? Just tell me what's on your mind. I really don't know how much longer I can take sitting here."

"Okay, here goes nothing. Brock Edwards called me today. He said the minute you heard the name, you'd know what it was all about. Something about June somebody and her daughter. Some Bunny lady came into his shop and really upset him. You know how emotional he can be."

"Only too well. Marc, I just don't see how this involves me. Besides, you know I never discuss my patients. Never."

"Okay, but Brock still thought you should know. He was afraid Angela wouldn't tell you, even though he asked her to. You know, I actually believe him on this one."

"Tell me what?"

"This customer, whoever it was that came to see Brock, said this June lady was convinced someone was trying to kill her, and that she shouldn't go home from the hospital. This Bunny was having husband troubles herself, so who knows? With some guy named Dan, I think. Brock said she was in tears for most of her appointment."

"Sounds like the ravings of a hysterical woman. If I were you, I'd pay no attention."

"Well, I wouldn't, except that Brock was so persuasive."

"Why didn't he call me himself?"

"He thinks you hate him."

"I do."

"Well, there it is. I suppose our discussion is over. You know, Eugene, it's not like you to let emotions rule your decisions. It's never happened before."

"My wife never left me for another man before either. But—and you can pass this on to Brock—I am adjusting to my new single life quite nicely. He need not worry about me, as I am not worrying about him, Angela, or anyone else."

"Right." Marc took a swig from his bottle and glanced around the smoky room. "So, do you see yourself getting back together with Angela?"

"Do you see yourself getting back together with Brock?"

"Okay, I deserve that. Look, it's getting late."

"Not really.

"It feels like it. Let's call it a night, shall we?"

Dr. Hart had barely made it to his car when his cell phone rang. It was going to be one of those nights. "Hello?"

"Eugene, it's Giles. Giles Dingwerth."

"Yes, Giles. How is June?"

"That's why I called, Eugene. She's dead."

"Dead! Are you sure? What happened?"

"You've got to come right away, Eugene. Please."

"I'll be right there." *And he thought the Green Parrot Lounge had been exciting.* He drove faster and faster, struggling to squelch the suspicions rising in his gut. He didn't want to believe his feelings. After all, he had no basis for accusations, no proof of foul play, and yet…deep down, if he trusted his instincts, he knew something was awry. He should have kept her in the hospital; he knew he shouldn't have let June Senior go home where it wasn't safe. Dr. Hart hadn't murdered her, yet still, he wondered.

Was he to blame?

Seventeen

After grabbing a rubbery hamburger in the hospital cafeteria, Dan trudged to the parking lot behind Ivymount Medical Center. A weary looking maintenance worker labored in the chilly December air, twining ropes of twinkling white lights around the wrought iron fence that surrounded the hospital. Distracted and tense, Dan ignored him, and admired the twinkling white lights. *It's holiday time, that special time of year when The Magic happens.* The shrill whine of an ambulance siren reminded him—magic discriminates. When it came to magic, only the chosen few were ever chosen. At least it seemed that way to Dan, especially these days. Something else bothered him, too.

Why did some people seem to taste the sweetness of Magic, while others simply dreamed of it? And some, like the unlucky soul who just arrived DOA in that ambulance there, just gave up, stopped believing, stopped hoping—time for an overdose of reality. Or, maybe he just never had a Plan.

Maybe, thought Dan, while he slid behind the steering wheel, *Plan* was just another word for magic. Maybe, there was no such thing as magic, or angels, or miracles, or "love at first sight." Only carefully laid, rational plans that either worked or didn't. Maybe June had been right all along, spouting her grim philosophy of life from her hospital bed. Happiness had escaped him.

He pulled onto the highway, headed for the Dingwerth compound. Dammit, he refused to surrender to Fate. Maybe June didn't believe in magic, but after Leila, he did. After his brush with the Angel of Hope, Dan still believed in miracles, despite the recent change in Leila's demeanor. No matter what she said, the magic between them had waned. Was it Giles or Carlos, or had she simple grown bored with him? Had Luther mentioned anything to her? He should have known better than to talk to someone he hardly knew about personal business. Now, a tangled mess loomed on his horizon. Perhaps Rocco knew something he didn't. He usually did, after all. He would call him tonight and he would know what to do. Now, he felt better. He had another Plan.

When he approached the Dingwerth residence, a stark reality emerged. What were all those cars doing there? If he didn't know better, he'd think June had died. Suddenly, his stomach felt bloated and heavy. He opened the car door and maneuvered his way through the mishmash of cars, parked on the winding drive to the front door.

He wondered if Bunny had arrived. He didn't see her car. Well, she just hadn't made it yet, that's all. Then, he heard it-the screech of tires behind him. He turned, and couldn't believe his eyes. Why was Leila driving Bunny's BMW? His heart racing; he felt frozen in place. The minute she opened her mouth, he knew.

"Danny, what do you think? Surprise!"

It certainly was, in so many ways.

"Lei—," he began, "I mean, Bunny, how is your mother? Did she make it home alright? I mean, why are all these cars here?"

Bunny shrugged. "Mommy likes to do things in grand style, Danny, you know that. Let's go in and see what she thinks of my hair. I'll bet she doesn't even know me. I don't even think you did. But, I'll bet Daddy will."

Giles! After what he'd overheard in Leila's hotel suite today, he would have to face Giles. At the mere suggestion, he began to sweat. In fact, despite his ambiguous feelings toward June, Giles' adulterous behavior disgusted him.

A passing glimpse in the ornate foyer mirror grounded him in the sobering reality. His recent performance ratings in the husband category were no better. If he included the contract for

Bunny's murder, well, they were worse, much worse—horrendous at best. Felicity dragged into the foyer, wearing a longer face than usual. She ought to at least pretend she was glad to see June. After all, everyone else did.

"Felicity," Bunny said, "is everything alright?"

"Did you not hear?" Felicity looked like she had just seen a ghost. Dr. Hart appeared behind her.

"Hear what?" Bunny said.

"Is June here?" Dan said. "Did she make it home?"

Dr. Hart stared through weary, soulful eyes. "I'm afraid she did." His shoulders slumped in submission.

"Wait till she sees my hair," Bunny said. "I just can't wait."

"I'm afraid you'll have to," Dr. Hart said, gazing past her into the street, at the waiting ambulance. "Bunny, I'm afraid there's a problem."

"But those guys don't seem to be in any big hurry," Bunny said. She glimpsed at two young paramedics strolling up the driveway.

Giles appeared in the arched doorway. "Bunns, Mommy isn't doing well at all. In fact...well, she may not be coming back."

"But she already did, didn't she? I don't get it, Daddy. What's going on?"

Looking back, the details of the following minutes would be blurred in Dan's mind. One thing he would never forget was his wife's hysteria: the wounded wail that escaped from her perfect mouth, the way she hugged June's limp body with determined strength, and finally, the way she implored him, Danny, to "...do something now, this minute, before Mommy dies." But someone, and Dan was convinced he knew who that somebody was, had beat him to the punch. In his jaded opinion that someone, this minute, could at least pretend to be grief-stricken.

Instead, Giles joked with the paramedics, holding the bedroom door for them, even—had Dan heard this correctly?—offering his casual commentary regarding the unseasonably mild winter. Once in June's bedroom, with Dr. Hart in command, Dan watched Giles excuse himself from the room. Felicity did the same, though Bunny asked the doctor if she might stay, and to Dan's amazement, he agreed.

Dan was more than happy to excuse himself, ostensibly for June's privacy, and this was not entirely unfounded. For, once he tiptoed out into the hall, and into the shadows, he observed Giles passing an envelope to Felicity. Dan's instincts told him to remain unnoticed. His instincts proved to be correct.

"I'm afraid this is the end, Felicity," he heard Giles say. "With June gone, I won't need you anymore."

"But Mr. Dingwerth, what about Miss Bolivar? Surely, she will need me."

"In all honesty, she doesn't like you. I know, I know, it's not fair. But, it's true. There's enough cash in that envelope to see you through for awhile. Now please, don't make this harder than it already is."

A scuffling sound in the hallway ended their conversation. It was the paramedics, toting a loaded stretcher. The lifeless mound that was once June Dingwerth now rested beneath a rumpled white sheet. The two men simply nodded as they nudged their way through the front door with Dr. Hart close behind.

"I'll meet you at Ivymount," he said to the driver. He gave the front door a slight shove and stepped onto the porch. "Goodbye Giles," he said, without turning to face him. I'll be calling you."

Giles simply nodded. Only Felicity displayed the slightest sign of distress. Did her tears belong to June or Giles?

Dan couldn't help but feel that Giles had picked a very bad time to fire Felicity. Besides, what was the rush? The sudden sight of Bunny, sporting her new Leila-inspired hair color, both alerted and sickened him. How much did Bunny actually know? Had she changed her hair color on a whim, as she had been known to do so many times before, or had someone, like that obnoxious reporter or her two meddlesome friends tipped her off? Perhaps worse, did Bunny know about her father's "engagement?"

He was almost certain she did not, and wouldn't believe him if he told her. No, if anyone would come out of this looking badly, it would be him, Dan Hunter. Giles would see to that, of that he was certain. He couldn't let that happen. From the corner of his eye, he caught a glimpse of a sobbing Felicity. She was making her way toward the front door. Hastily, he scribbled his cell phone number on the back of his business card. "Hey, Felicity," he whispered.

Startled, Felicity turned toward him. "*Sí?*"

"Give me a call, okay? I might know of a job for you."

Though she accepted the card, Felicity shook her head, even as she checked the street, presumably for a waiting car to take her home. "I think I will be leaving the city. And Mr. Hunter, so should you. Mr. Dingwerth, he is a very powerful man." She opened the door and the tiny woman trudged down the long driveway toward Rocco's waiting Mercedes.

Where was Giles? Where was Bunny? From the side hallway, he heard Giles' low voice. "Look Leila, Rocco will pick you up in a matter of minutes. Just be waiting for him. Don't make him wait. Right, Felicity is taken care of. Anyone who knew anything about us will be gone now, you know that, don't you? I didn't get where I am today by being careless."

Dan eavesdropped in the hall, disgusted. *No, your birthright into the Dingwerth Dynasty got you where you are today. What a lot of skill that required. And, what do you mean, they'll all "be taken care of?" Paid off? Eliminated? Just what is your plan, Giles Dingwerth IV?*

Bunny emerged from June's bedroom, sporting Leila's long, dark hair. In Dan's eyes, she suddenly appeared much older, less innocent, much sadder, less of a Bunny, and even less of a Leila. He simply did not know this stranger. The clock in the hall chimed eight times.

"Bunns," Giles said, slipping his cell phone into the breast pocket of his navy blazer, "you changed your hair color." His face wore a bemused expression, nothing more. Apparently, he saw no resemblance between his daughter and his lover. A chilly smugness infused his attitude. Dan found it abhorrent.

"Oh Daddy," she said, hurling herself into her father's arms. "What are we going to do now?"

For a second, Bunny's reaction puzzled Dan. He even felt a bit wounded. He wondered why his wife had not turned to him at such a distressful moment, and then, he demurred. Perhaps Bunny knew the kind of deceitful non-husband he had been during those past months. Her new hair color indicated as much. Could she have discovered his plans to end her life? The very thought chilled him to the core of his soul.

No, he decided, he didn't deserve Bunny's loyalty. If he wanted anything from her, he would have to earn it. What did Bunny think about Giles? Whatever nonsense was he spouting now?

"Well, Bunns," Giles said in a decidedly cool fashion, "we're going to have to carry on, just as the Dingwerths have always done. We have to be strong, the way Mommy would have wanted us to be. Remember her favorite saying?"

Bunny looked up at her father and wiped a tear from her eye. "You're as happy as you make up your mind to be—is that the right one?"

Giles nodded. "We have to make up our minds to be happy. Right, Daniel?"

Dan stared at the floor, but he couldn't help himself. His thoughts were focused on what June told him just hours before she died. Now, her words were etched indelibly in his mind: *"I should be happy. People tell me I should be, so I suppose I am."* Was June ever really happy? No, not in the way he wanted to be, Dan decided.

"Daniel? Are you alright? You know, I think it's a great tribute to the Junebug that you miss her so terribly. Why, I believe you miss her as much as Bunny and me."

"Do you miss her Mr. Dingwerth, sir?" Dan didn't know what had gotten into him. Like a bonfire, a fury blazed inside of him. Had Bunny not been present, he'd have spilled everything—Leila, Felicity, Rocco, and, of course, the engagement ring. Under the circumstances, how could he? The timing had been impeccable on Giles' part. Had he simply hoped June would die, or had he helped things along? Giles glared at him now, with an icy, judgmental glare on his lined face.

"You're very distraught right now. You know that, don't you? I've been meaning to ask you something for awhile now, and well, this might not be the perfect time for it, but here goes. How would you like to be the new President of Dingwerth Distinctive Designs?"

"Daddy!" Bunny said. "At a time like this…"

"Well, Bunns, life goes on, and like it or not, I'm not going to live forever. Daniel is as close to a son as I have, and while he's not a Dingwerth by blood, I know he'll stay right here and take good care of my daughter and my business, even after I'm gone. Isn't that right, Daniel?"

Trapped again. I'm trapped and should be happy, that's me. He searched Giles' face for a hint of shrewdness. Like a mask, an impossible-to-read mask, his face remained expressionless. "You talk as if you're leaving us, Giles."

"Are you going somewhere, Daddy?" Bunny said.

Giles barely flinched. "This has all been very sudden. I'll need some time to think. A man has to have a Plan. Don't you agree, Daniel?"

Dan considered Giles' smooth reply. "Of course." Somehow, he felt that Giles had arranged his Plan long ago, and the events of the day had unfolded on cue. It may have been sudden, but he had a sickening sense that June's death had been very much expected, at least by Giles. He couldn't explain it, but Dan felt an urge to protect Bunny from her father. They should return to their own home to consider Giles' most generous job offer, an offer that the patriarch seemed most anxious for Daniel to accept.

"Well, Daniel my boy, what do you think of my offer? You know, I really expected a more enthusiastic response from you. I am a bit disappointed. Bunns, tell him what a chance this is for him to rule the Dingwerth Dynasty from the top!"

To Dan's surprise, his wife hesitated. "I think he needs to think about it first, Daddy. You know, get used to the idea of all that power. Am I right, Danny?"

"Absolutely. It's a big step, Giles. For us both, really. You know, you should get used to the idea, too. We'll keep in touch. You ready to go, Hon?" The endearment felt strange on his tongue.

"Hon."

Dan had never called his wife anything other than Bunny, ever. What was happening to him, to her, to them? He was beginning to see a new future, with a new Plan. Maybe he could even see a life without any Plan, and yet he was feeling, well—happy. He strolled down the driveway to his car. Something else had changed. He hadn't thought about Leila at all that day, and for the first time since he met her, it just didn't matter.

Where in the devil was it? Giles tiptoed around the disheveled room, darkened by the dusky shadows. Utter stillness haunted the house, except for the chime of the massive grandfather clock in the grand foyer. Everyone—Eugene, Felicity, Bunny and Daniel—all of them behaved so strangely this afternoon. Why, they almost acted as if they didn't know him, and by God, they most certainly did. He was Giles Dingwerth IV, heir to the Dingwerth Dynasty and the luckiest widower in the world.

In the very near future, he would marry one of the most beautiful women in the world. He would be the envy of all of his friends at the Cinnabar Club, his aging friends who sat with their aging wives three times a week in silence while they ordered their early dinners. Such would not be his fate. He, Giles Dingwerth IV, had a Plan.

Where had it gone? Giles flung the fluffy, flowery bedspread on June's comfy queen-sized mattress to the floor. He dug into the mounds of pillows, searching. His heart began to pound faster, then stronger. *He needed to find it.* Perhaps paranoia had overwhelmed his sense of reason, but he couldn't allow a careless mistake to steal his future. *Where in the devil could it be?*

He didn't find it in the stuffy bedroom. Not until he reached the luxurious marble bathroom did it appear in all of its glory: the gold foil candy box, tied with a pink satin ribbon, flourished with a single pink polyester rose. He snatched it; its weightlessness shocked him. Lifting the lid, he discovered the reason. It was nearly empty—nearly. A few of the irresistible pink mints still remained.

He wondered if anyone, Eugene Hart for example, had seen the box. Felicity almost certainly had, but he'd been careful not to present it to June in front of her; just as he'd been careful to fill the box with June's favorite candy, those chalky, buttery pink mints. He never knew what made the pink ones better than, say the green or yellow ones, but Giles never had understood the Junebug. Never did and now, never would. Eugene would do his paperwork and find that June had broken her diet in the worst way, and it had proved fatal, oh well. No one would ever know Giles had asked poor depressed, diabetic June for a divorce just minutes before presenting her with a lethal dose of her favorite candy.

What else could he do? The time had come to tell her about Leila, Leila and his perfect romance, Leila and his perfect engagement. For a moment, Giles wondered how long he and Leila should wait before they married, and then, he remembered Carlos. Well, Leila would have to take care of that complication. That was all part of her part of the Plan.

Still, he thought it best to dispose of the candy box. No use leaving any evidence around for nosy people. He tucked the box under his arm and switched off the overhead light. He actually felt amazed that he didn't feel more guilt, more remorse, or more grief at June's passing. He concluded that June and his love for her had died long ago. When Bunny was five, he guessed it was. That was the day Bunny lost her first baby tooth, and he and June had argued, very bitterly he remembered now, about how much the tooth fairy should leave under Bunny's pillow. The former June Schulz had never experienced the gifts of the tooth fairy, while

Giles Dingwerth IV received at least five dollars a tooth, a child's fortune in the 1940's to be sure.

It was funny, wasn't it, how the little things could become so big. Well, one thing had led to another, and June accused Giles of wanting to spoil the young Bunny, while Giles accused his wife of depriving her, and somehow, the dispute melted into a chronic mudslinger regarding their respective and polar opposite socio-economic backgrounds. From that day forward, money and the blessing of a fictitious tooth fairy divided them. Giles stared at the gold foil box tied with the pink satin ribbon. Well, no matter now. He and Leila would not argue over money, the tooth fairy, or anything else. Their life together would be perfect.

He turned and surveyed the musty, cluttered room. Somehow, he sensed June's presence in the room with him right now, watching his every move. Oh, but that was ridiculous. No one ever questioned him, Giles Dingwerth IV, and if they did, why he would refuse to answer.

Still clutching the candy box, he rushed from the room.

Eighteen

Luther had been watching him now for oh, 'bout twenny minutes, that guy in the black Mercedes. He'd never liked the looks of that guy, not even when he first met him. Didn't trust anybody couldn't look him straight in the eye. The other thing was, why was he always driving that white-haired guy here and there? And it was always and all the time, man.

Luther wasn't entirely sure about this, but he was pretty damn sure this driver picked up somebody's girlfriend for 'em. He guessed it was most probably the white-haired guy. He'd seen her—that glamorous South-American model, Leila Boulivard, something like that, yeah. *Couldn't be that white guy with the pink Cadillac and the cute blond wife. Naw.*

He took a long swig of root beer from the amber bottle beside him. What do you know? There he goes now, driving an empty car. First time Luther had ever seen him do that. He rose from his seat in his office, and peered around the corner at the empty curb in front of the Hotel Charlotte. Yep, empty. Like his root beer bottle. *Hey.*

The following day...

Brock toyed with the leafy spinach salad set before him just seconds ago. The butterflies in his stomach told him what he needed to know. Why, they'd been there for the last three months, ever since he and Marc separated, ever since he'd decided to start a new life with Angela. Ah, Angela. How he had grown to resent her.

For a moment, he surveyed the bustling lunch crowd at the Café Charlotte, located in the hotel lobby. After all, Marc could be there, couldn't he? He worked there, didn't he? He had to eat, didn't he? Brock surely hoped he wasn't back on the liquid diet. Marc had gotten so scrawny on nothing but frothy cherry vanilla Slimshakes. Yuck.

He bit into his salad and winced. Onions. He had asked the waiter to please leave out the onions. Please. He wasn't good with onions, just like he wasn't good with caffeine and bee stings, and oh my—there he was, strolling into the lobby looking better than ever—it was Marc.

Just in time to ruin the view, along comes that nervy reporter. What was her name? Gumby? A rain cloud dashed Brock's sunny mood. What if, oh what if Marc had started a new life with Gumby in his absence? He dropped his fork while he watched them embrace. Well after all, Brock thought, he'd been the one to leave Marc, hadn't he? If Marc had simply moved on without him, it was only what he deserved.

Perhaps he should just leave. Leave without even talking to Marc. Well, either way, he had to know how Marc felt about him. Not knowing was pure torture. Just like his life with Angela had been. That's right, had been. Angela was so o-v-e-r. He'd spent the last two nights in the hair color room at the shop, camped out on a lumpy cot. It was no use. Marc was the only one for him. Oh look, Gumby was leaving!

He pulled a twenty-dollar bill from his Gucci wallet and slid it under his bread and butter plate. Here comes the waiter now. He would forget about the onions. He felt as fabulous as he looked. Simply put, it was time to go!

Stepping out of the café, he checked his reflection in the lobby mirror. He was pleased. His golden highlights were fresh, only a week old, and he had managed to lose somewhere in the neighborhood of ten pounds since Marc had last seen him. Not to mention his new pleated silk trousers and custom monogrammed silk shirt. A herringbone gold chain encircled his neck. He was looking outrageously fine.

Marc saw him first. But no matter. Brock knew in an instant. He had come home. He recalled a story he'd once heard about an extraordinary, yet restless, butterfly. A man had tried to capture the butterfly, but to no avail. It had escaped. But, the man was advised that if the butterfly flew away and never came back, it had never really belonged to him in the first place, but, if it chose to return, it would remain with him forever.

Now, at this very second, that is how he felt about Marc. He was the restless butterfly that had escaped and had returned of his own free will. Perhaps he needed to leave to return to Marc—this time, forever.

Eugene Hart had seen a lot of things in his life so far, but tonight, well, he believed the news he had received tonight topped the list of "Weird Things I Want to Forget." For him, that list was growing longer and looser. Not a good sign for a guy who would very much like to retire. Now on his way to his former residence to deliver the divorce papers to his soon to be ex-wife, he had some spare time to analyze the meaning of it all.

For starters, June's laboratory report had indicated that Mrs. June Dingwerth, a sixty-three year old female and serious diabetic, had ingested a massive, lethal amount of sugar immediately preceding her death. Once again, she had broken her diet. He would have accepted this without hesitation, except for the one troubling issue. June's question still lingered in his mind like a moldy cobweb in an attic: "Is it safe for me to go home?"

Now, he chided himself for dismissing such a disturbing remark. It should have disturbed him, it should have spurred him to investigate further, but wait a minute—it was all coming back to him. He'd had a word with Giles, and he'd had a word with June too, and asked her if she wanted to talk about her "unsafe" feelings. Asked her why she'd told him that her apparent sudden death, if it should happen, might not be an accident. And she'd said, "I really can't remember why."

Upsetting, yes, deeply disturbing; but, all circumstantial. Should he insist on a criminal investigation? The Dingwerths were high profile, influential people. All he had were lots of gut feelings, and no hard evidence. He had discharged June Dingwerth, and she broke her diet yet again, one too many times. It was bound to happen sooner or later. Such events were the stuff of everyday life, were they not?

Speaking of troubling events, here he was now, approaching the curb in front of his house. He still thought of it that way, and guessed he always would. After all, he'd designed the two story brick Colonial with the slate roof and copper gutters, and he was still paying for it, wasn't he? Gazing at it from the street, he was still proud of it, still attached to it, still felt like it was a part of him; much like the feelings he had for Angela, an admission he would acknowledge only to himself.

He didn't even need to ring the doorbell. The stained oak door cracked open and Angela appeared. He had forgotten how beautiful he still found her. Gripping the divorce papers in his right hand, he stopped himself from embracing her. *Was he crazy?*

"Hi there, Eugene," Angela said. "It's too cold to talk out here. Come inside for a second?"

"I don't think that would be a good idea with Brock and all of that, Angela. I'll just…"

"He's gone."

"When will he be back?"

"He won't, Eugene." She glanced over his shoulder. A tear dripped from her eye and she brushed in away in haste. "It's… it's over."

An awkward pause followed while the doctor considered his next move. The frosty air stung his cheeks, and he ached to escape the bitter wind. Well, and why not? After all, it was still his house. He had a right to be there. "I think I will come in for a few minutes, if you don't mind."

"You can take your coat off."

Was it his imagination, or was Angela flirting with him? After the day he'd had, he decided, anything was possible.

"Just give it to me," she continued, "and I'll put it upstairs on the bed." Angela turned and winked. "When I come back, I'll make us both a drink. Still take Scotch and water on the rocks?"

"Sure." Well, this was a surprise. Surprise? No, it was a major shock, that's what it was. He watched his wife trot up the wide stairs. Did he want her back? After all they had been through together? Even after Brock? She mixed the drinks now, clad in a gold lameé jumpsuit that hugged all of her well placed curves. Hardly what one would consider "breakup attire."

"So sweetie, what brings you by this time of the evening?" She sat across from him and crossed her long legs.

Sweetie? Angela had always had great legs. Still did. He sipped his drink. *It was perfect, like those sweet legs of hers.* "I brought the divorce papers, remember? You asked me for them a couple of weeks ago. I thought you'd be anxious to have them, so here I…"

Her lips were on his, her arms were around his neck, her long legs encircled his waist, what—what was happening to him? "Angela," he said between breaths, "what are you doing?"

"Eugene, put your drink down."

He did.

"What do you mean, she's not there?" Giles said.

He had nearly finished packing his golf clothes, and was getting ready to tackle his tailored suits. A man had to get married in an expensive suit, didn't he? And now, here was Rocco, telling him he had returned without his fiancée.

"Rocco, you're not making any sense. Explain yourself."

Rocco simply shrugged. "Miss Bolivar is gone. Poof!"

"What is poof?"

"That's what the desk clerk at the hotel, he tell me. He say Miss Bolivar, she check out in the middle of the night."

"What is his name? I'll have him fired!"

"Hmmm…let me remember. It was Marc. Marc Stephen. No,

it was Stephens Marc."

"Well, which is it?"

"Mr. Dingwerth, sir, it does not matter. Miss Bolivar, she is gone."

"Well, she must have left a message, or a note, or a, a ring..." Giles' voice trailed off into a whisper. Rocco lowered his head. He dared not look up at this exact moment.

"No sir, she left nothing. Nothing at all."

"But I'm Giles Dingwerth the fourth!" His voice crackled with emotion. "Rocco, you must do something."

"There is nothing to do, sir."

Excitement overwhelmed Gabby at this moment. This luscious scoop would rocket the Gateway Gabette to wuthering heights! Well, maybe not wuthering, but higher, okay? Of course, she'd heard the rumors, just like everybody else that patronized Beauty by Brock. Old man Dingwerth's Latina mistress dumped him for some better, younger, richer, guy, and he wanted, indeed needed to leave town. Everyone was talking, gossip was swirling, June's death sure had been convenient, hadn't it?

And now, Giles Dingwerth IV wanted to pass the Dingwerth Dynasty to his son-in-law, Daniel Hunter. How she managed to get this interview was still something of a mystery to her. One day, Marc called her and it was hers, just like that. She'd never thought she'd find herself sitting in this office ever again, and now, here she was, face to face with the heir apparent, Daniel "The Donut Man" Hunter. "So Mr. Hunter, how does it feel to be the new President of Dingwerth Distinctive Designs?"

Dan leaned back in his leather chair. "Great, Gabby, just great."

"The Dingwerths have had quite a commotion in their family lately. Care to comment?" By the look on Dan's face, she knew. She had crossed the proverbial line. Now, she would take a step back.

"No." He leaned forward and whispered. "We're off the record now, okay? Here's what you print. Giles has retired after losing his beloved wife of thirty eight years, his only child June

Dingwerth Hunter is expecting a baby in November, and his son-in-law, Daniel J. Hunter, that's me, is the new President of Dingwerth Distinctive Designs."

"That's all?"

"That's all there is to it."

"Ho, ho, ho. We both know better."

"Better is the enemy of best, is it not? It's been a pleasure. Call me anytime, and I'll tell you what to print. Now, shall I show you the door, or shall I phone security?"

Dan found he was indeed a changed man. Not because of his sudden promotion, or his pending fatherhood. No, it was Giles himself who had changed him. Giles and his plans, Giles and his schemes, and Giles' deception opened Dan's eyes. In Giles, he saw himself, not only in the present, but in the next thirty or so years. He didn't want to end his career as an imposter. Whatever he would be, he would be the real thing.

Leila disappeared as quickly as she appeared, just like a dream. Dan supposed that's what she was, and all she was ever meant to be, at least for him, and certainly for Giles as well. Sometimes, he worried about Giles, as depressed and lonely as he had become, but although he didn't spend as much time at the Cinnabar Club as he once did, he seemed to enjoy his bridge club once a week. He didn't sell the Dingwerth residence, nor did he leave it much.

And Bunny? Well, besides her pregnancy, her hair color changed immediately. At her very next appointment, she returned to her "natural" blonde shade, Scandinavian Sunset No. 9. Love at first sight? Bunny had always believed in it, from the first day she met Danny. It was just like her mother said it was for her when she first met her Daddy.

Daddy taught Bunny everything she needed to know about getting what she wanted. "Never forget, Bunnykins," he said while gazing into the distance, "you must always have a Plan." Bunny replied that she always had a Plan, Daddy. For the rest of her life, Bunny had a Plan. She always got what she wanted—and that never changed.

Claire Applewhite is a graduate of St. Louis University, where she earned an AB in Communications and an MBA, Finance, and completed the Mercantile Leadership Program for Women. A past participant in the Summer Writers Institute at Washington University, she is a contributing writer for the St. Louis Post-Dispatch. Her first mystery novel, *The Wrong Side of Memphis,* was released in May 2009, by L&L Dreamspell. A short story, *Moonlight Becomes You So,* was released in June, 2009, also by L&L Dreamspell. *Unchain My Heart,* a romantic thriller, was recently named a Semi-Finalist in the Faulkner Creative Writing Competition. In 2009, she organized **Rouge et Noir, LLC.** Visit www.Claireapplewhite.com for details.

Claire is a current Board member of the Midwest Mystery Writers of America and the Missouri Writers Guild, where she is the current Vice-President and Conference Chair for the Annual 2010 Conference. Claire is an active member of the St. Louis Metropolitan Press Club, St. Louis Writers Guild, Sisters in Crime, Heartland Writers Guild and Mystery Writers of America.

LaVergne, TN USA
06 July 2010
188485LV00002B/1/P